Flowers In The Concrete

Short Story Collections

"They buried us, but they didn't know we were seeds"
- Dinos Christianopoulos

A Dedication To...

This book is dedicated to every Black woman who has impacted my life. My love for Black women developed when I was three years old. My mother did hair out of her apartment. I remember seeing black women of all types with a mixture of personalities and physical attributes. This book is dedicated to those Black women. Black queens who didn't know they were queens. All of the queens that made an impression on my life for the better, I thank you all. This book is dedicated to my grandmother, the beloved Gloria Jean Taylor. This book is Dedicated to my sisters, Glenyshia, Kanika, and Julissia. Rest in Paradise to my sister Erica. This is a dedication to my nieces, Kamari, Paris, Nakendra, Carmela, Nayla, and Natalie JeanL (when they are old enough to understand). And last but not least this book is dedicated to me, because I am a flower that bloomed from the concrete despite all of those odds that were stacked against me.

Contents

Black Supremacy…………..…...pg. 4-44
Trippin' Like A MF…..pg. 45-102
Black Amarucan Queens…pg. 103-153
Black Girls Are Kings………..pg. 154-215
Flowers In The Concrete….pg. 216-277
A Ghetto Sci-Fi……..278-312

BLACK SUPREMACY

By

Damita Taylor

Chapter I

There are some things that will never change. Like Golden hitting the Shoot in his all black tailored velvet suit, and myself Swag Walking to Lil Baby Woah in my tailored black dress and red bottom heels. King Jerome, our big brother's personal DJ, kept us hype from the DJ booth as he shouted adlibs over the microphone. That was me and Golden's special tradition. Since he was a toddler. He and I would have mini dance battles against each other. The event planner sashayed throughout the ballroom making sure the decorators were on point with the finishing touches for my father's Black is Excellence Gala which started in less than thirty minutes. The servers were setting up serving trays and preparing drinks for the arriving guests. The sweet aroma, expensive perfumes, cologne, top notch southern cooking, and the rare scent of wealth surrounded the air like a soaring dove.

"AYEEE. YEAH. YEAH. BOW. BOW. OOOUU." King Jerome hollered over the mic, making me and Golden feel like we were doing more damage on the dance floor than we actually were.

"Listen bruh the Shoot ain't got a damn thing on the Swag Walk. My era was just flyer than yours."

Golden waved me off and Hit Them Folks with a Woah to top it off. I laughed then Walked it Out. Golden threw his head back laughing too hard for my ego. I couldn't have my brother who thought I was the coolest woman to ever walk the earth laugh at me like a joke.

"What's funny big head boy?"

" You, mane you look like somebody drunk aunt doing that dance." Golden said, still tripping. I kept right along with my Jig. Nothing wrong with drunk aunties, and some dances just never go out of style.

SJ walked in with so much fucking audacity I could've spat in his face. He whispered something in King Jerome's ear which made him cut the music.

"Foreal SJ, what the fuck bruh?" Golden asked, trying to mean mug but his babyface wasn't monstrous enough to intimidate our big brother.

"Man stop crying, I gotta make sho' my sound right before my set tonight. Y'all can rock out to this fye I'm bringing or get the fuck on somewhere."

Golden and I walked over to one of the high tables. "Trash ass nigga." Golden said loud enough for SJ to hear him.

SJ clenched his jaws and scrowled, "Suit yourself." He said, then hopped on the microphone. "CHECK. CHECK. YEA. YEA. Money go so easy, these hoes be too easy, all I ever I trusted is god and my glock, on god and my glock umma be the end of you niggas. Assuming umma lick is what's hindering you niggas, and I'm so fuckin' blessed it's offending you niggas, you broke and you sad get out cha feelings lil nigga..."
Golden shook his head. "Fucking studio gangsta, he don't know shit about the streets." He said then checked his phone. One of his little friend girls messaged him some words that switched his whole mood. A look of both sadness and innocence circled inside his eyes. The server offered us a mini plate of stuffed crab cakes. As we both ate, I decided to pick his brain. Never mind SJ, it never took us long to tune him out.

"What's holding you baby bruh?" I asked. Golden smirked. I knew he was ready to downplay any

6

heavy emotion that he truly felt, so I made it easy for him.

"Who's the lucky girl?"

"Amore. A new girl around the way, but she's so different sometimes she confuses me."

"Hm, she sounds like a challenge. I'm intrigued."

"She's dope, lookwise, body, brains, all that but she a lil too difficult."

"What's wrong with that, easy come easy go? You should be happy she isn't one of these fast girls out here getting smashed and trashed by every other nigga."

The smirk dropped away. Golden hung his head. I tilted it upright with my diamond studded fingernail. He exhaled.

"Daddy told me it's never good for a man who loves a woman more than that woman loves him. And if he does find himself loving that woman more than she loves him than that fool better find two other women to help him love her at a distance." Golden said.

"What kind of pimp shit is that?" I asked.

Golden smirked bashfully. "That man said cause one of the bitches gone be nastier enough to keep you out of her, and the other one'll be money hungry enough to keep you busy spending your time and money elsewhere."

My mouth dropped, my pops was a smooth one *King Penny Dropper*, so I shouldn't have been surprised by the game he threw Golden. I guess because Pops had grown into such a prestigious gentleman, rubbing shoulders with mayors, some of the world's most prominent lawyers and business people. He began taking courses in socioeconomics, and even leveling up in his yoga practice. Not to mention I hadn't heard that man curse in years. It was hard to hear Golden, who did one helluva impression of my pops, reciting the playa' proverb my pops had slid him. But please believe I wasn't no sucker for love my damn self. Plus, after witnessing my mother 's foul ways towards him, I didn't blame my father for hardening his heart towards love and women. I wasn't offended by a long shot.

"That's some good advice, why didn't you take it?"

" I did, but it doesn't feel good to break her heart sis."

"What do you mean?" I asked nibbling on a crab cake.

"The girl I love just texted me that she knows I've been cheating on her, but I was only cheating to avoid all the love I had for her. She broke up with me, now I lost her for good."

Golden was sincerely hurt, and although I loved my baby bruh, I couldn't help but laugh. "Look Gold, she's a girl. Sweet talk her, buy her some shit, make her forgive you since you want her back so bad."

"If I get her back I'm never hiding my feelings again."

"You right Gold, all girls aren't the same, and should be treated accordingly. If you straight up with your lil bae she might understand."

"You think so."

"I know so."

I nudged his jaw softly and he smiled.

"Blood of my blood, flesh of my flesh. Nothing makes a man prouder than witnessing his offspring expressing unbound love and respect for each other." Pops said as he emerged with Jasmine's arm wrapped into his.

"Everyone looks dapper and gorgeous tonight, how about a family portrait?" Jasmine asked, and my father nodded at her suggestion.

"SJ, come join the photo mane." Pops said. SJ waved my father off and kept fiddling with the mic. He was so fucking selfish. Just like our mother. That's why I couldn't stand him.

"SJ, you can get back to that but we're getting this photo as a family right now." Pops said with more authority than before.

SJ left the mic on the DJ table and came over to us with the sourface. Pops hugged me and SJ close to him, his eldest son and only daughter. I held on to Golden and Golden hugged Jasmine. The event photographer snapped us up and that was that.

All the guests had arrived. A lot of exchanges of laughter, ideas, profound networking, and shared admiration. The cooking was on point too. I had a slight buzz from the Krug Grande Cuvee

10

champagne. A live band serenaded us with the saxophones, snares, and all that smooth jazz. I was at my father's side, the whole night. He was proud of me. Not only was I book smart. A year away from receiving my master's in entertainment law. I also had the gift of gab. The old heads loved my charm and respected my drive. Pops and I had the gaze and the grin of Councilwoman Sheneka Taylor. She stood out with her short red bob and long silky black dress. A slender cinnamon skin woman.

"Empress, what is it like being the daughter of such a brilliant leader in media production, and a stellar capitalist might I add?" Councilwoman Taylor asked.

"My father's a man first, and all that he is lives on within me. As far as I see it, I am proud of all his accomplishments, but in all actuality he's just hitting the marks that will fulfill our family's legacy, and me, well I'm set and ready for the torch he passes on."

"Wonderfully put Ms. Empress."

"Wonderfully asked, Councilwoman."

Councilwoman and I made a toast, we chuckled as our glasses clinked, and she winked at me as we both sipped our champagne. There was an art to conversing with sharks. Pops had taught me the ropes at six years old. *"Hold your head high, relax your shoulders, stare 'em dead in the eyes, and make sure your every word is strong and sharp. That'll be your winning ticket into the heart of a shark."* But don't get it twisted unlike vultures, sharks don't play dirty, sharks play without fear. Just another gem from Pops treasure box of knowledge and wisdom. Maybe it was because I was a daddy's girl, maybe I was just an old soul who honored the ones who honored and valued me. I don't know, whatever the imbalance was in the way I carried myself as a twenty-four year old woman versus the way SJ carried himself as a twenty seven year old man. Had drawn a wedge between our siblingship. SJ was a liability to all that my father had built.

SJ the fucking embarassment, struted, or should I say staggered around the gala with a half empty bottle of Cognac, promoting his socials on a cheaply done business card. Wearing a Versace shirt with the top buttons undone like some 2Pac wannabe. Fuck what you heard, no amount of wealth and proper raising can teach class. My poor excuse of a brother was sent into the world a damn fool, and that's a damn shame. While I politicked and parlayed alongside my father, I kept a keen eye on the shit show that was waiting to happen on the behalf of his first born.

As the night progressed, there were a few performances from well respected musicians. Pops hand selected and booked artists such as Anthony Hamilton, Don Trip, Playa Flyy, K. Michelle, and Leela James. SJ walked back and forth from the DJ booth to the bar. I could tell he was anxious, moreso for his performance. All the Cognac he drank sweated through his pores.

"...And last but most definitely not least ladies and gentlemen, the next guest is creating a lane for himself outside of his dad's shadow, this man here is a hot spitta and plenty of competition for the young independent rappers coming up in the M-Town. Ladies and gentlemen give it up for Sir Tha Savage," King Jerome introduced SJ from his booth.

A few cheered. Several applauded. Even still the moment SJ touched the mic and the beat dropped, dude lost all composure. SJ smacked the ass of one female server and tipped her from a money stack in his skin tight jeans that hung off his ass. It wasn't enough that he stood out like a sore thumb, he had to go against the grain even further by walking into the faces of our guests dancing and rapping his song noone knew the words to. SJ, like my father, was dark as cocoa and unlike my father he wore bukoo chains, a mouth filled with golds , and a head full of purple rope twists. A deadbeat father of three girl children by three different women. One in North Memphis, one in Orange Mound, and the other one in Arkansas. It's unfortunate to say but I can't remember a day that I ever looked up to my older brother in a respectful and admirable way. And even though he envied my many accomplishments he had no choice but to respect the stature of the true solid woman I've become. More than that though, I could read right through SJ. He wanted to be the captain so bad, but Pops was the captain which made me lieutenant. I was the son my father expected SJ to be. It was oh so clear who would carry the torch to lead on my father's empire, and that ate SJ up inside.

   SJ had some of the young ones' ears with the trap beat. They bobbed their heads and did their instagram choreographed type dances. Golden stood back with an obvious look of annoyance. SJ jumped wildly into the air, but dropped his bottle of cognac and busted his ass on the come down. The young ones recorded and laughed. Except Golden who walked away fed up with the whole situation. SJ was embarrassed and slammed the mic on the floor. From the balcony to the foyer of the ballroom I could see the disgust on many of the guests' faces. SJ stormed out of the gala and onto the circular black stone driveway lined with foreign cars. I was right behind him. He headed swiftly toward his Benz.

"You can't run from every mess you make, SJ." I said to the back of him.

SJ swung around and his body jerked to the side as he rushed to my face. "What the fuck you just say to me?" SJ asked, spraying his venomous rage into my face.

"You heard what I said, nigga. You're a chump and a disgrace to this family."

SJ towered over me with hunched shoulders and gritted teeth. In heels I was five-nine while SJ stood at six-five in his Louis Vuitton flats alone. His beastly stature didn't intimidate me. After all God had sent a child to cut down the head of a giant, and giants do fall. Simply put, SJ had the height, but I had all the heart and grace.

"Who you supposed to be? If I was a different type of man I'd smack the shit of you just to put your hoe ass in your place."

"Nigga please, the only reason I show your useless ass mercy is because of our father. Remember that." I said then pushed him hard enough to make his drunk ass hit the ground once again. SJ growled at me, but I was done with him. It was clear where the two of us stood with each other.

It was well past midnight. I sat on the outdoor balcony with Pops. We smoked cigars. A little tradition we shared after every win no matter if it was a big win or small win.
" Did I ever tell you the story about Grandpop Chuck?" Pops asked. I shook my head no.

"Well when your Grandpop was ten years old his daddy took him up to Harlem to experience a Malcolm X conference in the flesh. Here he was, this ten year old boy from musty ass Georgia with an opportunity to witness the black Messiah speak life back into dead people. Grandpop said that very day he decided that he would be his own master."

"I thought that was the only way to live and thrive in this world. It's not like he had any other choice."

"That's true, but he was ten years old, Daughter. Imagine that. But as the story went on, Grandpop told me he went back to Macon Georgia with a plan. He said that there were two things he needed to do. One get a job. The other buy a camera. He worked his way up to both and became one of the youngest photographers to ever do it, and black at that."

"Dope story. I love to hear our family history, but what's your point?"

"The point is your Grandpop. My daddy took those pictures and began his own magazine company called Black and Gifted, in the early sixties. He was ten years old. In those magazines he printed quotes from Malcolm X speeches on every picture of black people and any form of black culture he captured."

Pop's message was finally getting through to me. Grandpop was his inspiration. Although Grandpop never owned nothing more than a fruit truck as far as business is concerned, he planted a lifetime of seeds for the generations after him.

Pops continued, " One night Grandpop was out in the city snapping pictures on a sunday. He was so tuned into the images he was catching on his camera that he crossed over the wrong side of the tracks..." Pops said.

I listened, mellowed out not only from the buzz the cigar gave me, but also from all the champagne I'd drank earlier that night. Pops always told interesting stories passed down from Grandpop and Big Momma, some were funny, most of them were serious family jewels. Pops told me that Grandpop ended up in a secluded rural type neighborhood where there were more trees and land than houses and businesses. Although Grandpop was fearless, he wasn't foolish. He had a gut feeling that somebody was watching him. Grandpop trusted his gut, but he didn't want to make the wrong move by being reactive instead of proactive. The neighborhood was strange. Grandpop had never been on that side of town before, so he assumed like many cautious black folk that it was a whites only neighborhood. He braced himself to be rushed by the kkk, the police, or some plain evil racist. His heart raced, though he kept a calm demeanor. Grandpop walked past one house and these bright strobe lights blinded him. Grandpop was about to strike out running when he ran into a man. A blueberry black man that had a jumbo curly afro and had his skin tight shirt that said *Black Supreme* tucked into his khakis, smiled down at Grandpop.

"Say young chile, where you gunning to?" The man asked Grandpop

"I'm lost sir." Grandpop answered wide eyed and terrified.

"Why, thanks chile. Sir is the highest form of respect you can give when addressing a black man ." The man said then reached out his hand to shake Grandpop's hand.

"What's your name chile?" he asked.

"Charles, but my folks call me Chuck."

"You's a brave soul lil baby, out here all alone like this, but fear not. I'll get you home."

"Really? Thank you sir."

"Oh, don't you give me no praise. Every black chile on this earth is a chile of mine, it's my duty as a black man to serve you, and to teach ya cause ain't nothing in this world for free. So I'll get ya home and you get to give me this here fine camera of yours."

Pops said Grandpop was devastated but grateful all the same, because he had his life and a valuable lesson to leave with.

"Everything comes with a price." Pops said. "Everything." He said. I understood his meaning. Yet he still went on to say, " Because of your mother I have you, but then there's SJ who'll probably be the death of me." Pops said, and that sent chills down my back.

"Not on my time." I said. Pops smiled. I kissed his cheek. "Goodnight Pops, I love you old man."

"I love you more my Empress, go ahead and get you goodnight's rest." Pops replied.

"Yes Sir." I said, and he laughed.

After showering the day's dirt away, I sat in a robe at my vanity inside my bedroom. I wrapped my hair, and used makeup wipes to make sure the dirt and oil from the makeup I'd worn that night was fully cleaned from my face. I fell asleep in the process, and dreamt of my mother. We were riding horses across the land like old times. Racing. My mother and I were both excellent horse riders, and we loved to compete. Back then she always won since she knew the land better than I did. As I got older though I began to keep up with her, and even in my dream we were neck and neck as we halted our horses at the lake.

" I loved your father to death. He was my first and only love." My mother said with tears streaming from her eyes. First of all I'd never heard my mother say the word love to my father, so her confession of her undying love for my father put me in total shock, but the tears definitely blew me away. Mind you my mother is alive and well. She just abandoned us after she divorced my father ten years ago. In ten years I'd spoken to my mother twice and both encounters ended horribly. The woman was a diva stuck in her ways. She'd milked her meal ticket long enough and took off to enjoy her a lifetime of vacations. The same way she took off on her horse in my dreams and left me alone by the lake, confused and taken aback.

"Empress. Empress. Wake up. Wake up sis!" Golden was shaking me back to reality. I awoke sweaty and panicked.

"Wha-- What's happening?" I asked sleepily.

"Pop's been shot. He's dead." Golden said. His voice cracked and squealed.

That shocked feeling my mother left me with never went away. I stared at me and Golden's reflection through my vanity mirror. I thought I was still dreaming. My whole world felt unreal at that moment. I couldn't cry. I couldn't scream. All I could do was be still, because there was no way my father went out like that.

"I just kissed him goodnight." I said. Golden hugged me tight. His eyes were flooded with tears.

"The ambulance hasn't arrived yet. We have to sit with him." Golden said, his voice trembled and cracked. I nodded, and tied my robe shut.

Jasmine hadn't had the privilege of getting herself dressed decently. She cried horrifically at my father's side in her panty and bra. Blood seeped from the burning hole in his chest. His body was still warm. I imagined his newly released spirit hovering over us. Just as shocked and saddened as us. No, I didn't believe God called my father home. I wasn't trying to hear any of that philosophical bullshit. Somebody had murdered my dad. They'd stolen my hero from me. My nightmare had only just begun.

CHAPTER II

When the ambulance and crime unit arrived, our home became an official crime scene. They chalked a trace of my father's slain body before a white sheet was thrown over him. Number blocks were placed around the balcony and throughout the estate. My father's body was airlifted to the corona.

Two investigators sat us down in the family room. Golden gave Jasmine a blanket to cover herself. Her eyes were soulless like she was having an outer body experience. Golden and I are my father's children. We were broken inside but we held it together.

"I give you all my deepest condolences, I can imagine how difficult this may be for you right now. Please understand as draining as it may be your full cooperation will be the key to getting your father the justice he deserves." Sgt. Wells said.

Ironically he looked as stressed as we were. Droopy bags hung under his eyes. He massaged his temples tenderly. His clothes were wrinkled, yellow stains seeped from the armpit of his shirt. His notebook was worn as if toted it for years. The pages fell from the spirals. Detective Charles was an older man. Standoffish. Emotionally detached from our travesty. He sat astute, discreetly observing our luxurious decor.

"Would you like something to drink? Water, sweet tea…?" I asked. My father had taught me to always show hospitality to those we welcomed in our home, and although it was under an unfortunate circumstance, Sgt. Wells and Detective Charles were guests in our home.

"Water would be great." Detective Charles responded.

"Sweet tea for me please. I'm a southern boy." Sgt. Wells replied.

When I returned with the beverages, Detective Charles was browsing the curation of family portraits on our wall. I handed him his water and he commented, "There's three of you." I wasn't fully present so his comment went over my head.

Yes, me Jasmine and Golden. That's three. He must've seen my indifference towards his remark, so he added, "You have another brother." Detective Charles pointed to SJ' photo.

"Yeah, SJ he hasn't been home since the party last night." I said.

"So he lives here?"

"Yeah, we all do."

"I see."

I gave Sgt. Wells his sweet tea, and sat next to Golden. He was rocking side to side, bouncing his knees something ferocious. The reality of it all was kicking in. Our father was in heaven now. He was never coming back. The mansion felt cold and empty, even though it was filled with some of the world's most lavish furniture and material wealth. The sergeant drank the sweet tea gratefully.
"Thank you very much ma'am. I didn't know how bad I needed that." Sgt. Wells said. I flicked my hand. It was time to get down to business. Afterall the detectives were there for a job.

"Alright sergeant, what do you need to know?" I asked.

"Can each of you recount your last moments with Mr. Black before the shooting?"

"We smoked our victory cigar and I kissed him goodnight." I said.

"I didn't know that would be my last time seeing Pops so I dapped him up and went to my end of the crib to shower and play the game." Golden said.

Jasmine said nothing. She was a zombie, zoned out from the world around her. The detectives knew better than to pressure her for a statement. So they continued asking Golden and I questions.

"Did Mr. Black have any enemies?"

"Any significant conflict in the past months?"

"Where were you at the time of your father's murder?"

"What were his last words?" .... So on and so forth.

As the questioning went on the further I felt from my father. I was tempted to call him. To ask him, but I knew that was impossible, therefore their questions were unanswerable. The detectives left around three am. I sat awake staring at the bleak grey sky through the glass ceiling. My entire existence was an open wound. I had never felt so vulnerable. The world. The reality. I once knew, breathed, lived, and felt was fading. My life was like sand and my hand was the hourglass, because I was losing touch of everything that made me me in a matter of seconds.

The following days were hectic. The news of my father's murder was plastered on every online media blog site, CNN, and all other major news platforms both locally and nationwide. It'd been days since I've eaten or slept. My focus was preparing my father's eulogy along with his obituary. The funeral would be the following Saturday, but my head and shoulders were weighed down by strain and the madness surrounding me. My uncle Majesty flew in to help me with the funeral arrangements. Golden had been locked up in his room since the night of Pop's murder. Since then we'd spoken only once, and neither of us could stop the tears from falling. Jasmine had slept for days on end. She complained of an excruciating headache, and swore she may be suffering symptoms of a heart attack. I told her to drink more water, because more than likely she was dehydrated from crying all those tears. But of course to be on the safe side her personal physician came to the estate to check her physical health and prescribed her a moderate dosage of percocets and urged her to rest and stay hydrated.

Uncle Majesty was my backbone through the whole process. He was younger than Pops by one year but he had a head and chin full of gray. Blindness in one eye caused him to have one bluish gray eye and one light brown eye. An odd looking yet beautiful dude. He made sure that Pop's suit was tailored to the tee. We both agreed on a white suit with soft blue stripes. Laying my father to rest was very sentimental for the both of us. Of course Pops was going out in style. He was a king, so that was a given. But on a bigger note we needed the funeral to be about his legacy. No cameras, no celebrity attention, only close family and friends would be in attendance. My father was a man of silent faith. He still attended his late mother and father's first baptist church in North Memphis, and was a generous giver to the church. It was only right to have the funeral there.

The night before the funeral I had a terrible nightmare. It scared me awake. The context of the nightmare was so vivid that I wasn't sure if it was a bad dream or premonition. That pain I felt was too real for it to be some random dream. I'll spare the details for now, since I can't stomach the thought.

SJ had been high off lean and pills from days on end. Whenever I spoke to him he was barely coherent. The dude was a pitiful sight, more pitiful than ever before.

Unc gathered us at the dining table for breakfast. Though no one had an appetite or could stomach any food even if we tried, Unc felt it was mandatory for us to prepare our minds as a unit before we had to share our pain with outsiders. We were a living, breathing portrait of the sorrow that forms when the backbone of the family dies. SJ wore sunglasses. Golden stared sadly at the seat at the head of the table. Jasmine, oh Jasmine. She struggled to stir her own cup of coffee. Her hand shook violently. She was clearly on edge. I sat with a sick uneasy feeling in my gut. The residue from the nightmare still lingered in my heart and mind. Unc stirred Jasmine's coffee for her. She smiled at him bashfully and tilted her head to him.

" A lot on the line right now. A lot of changes are in motion and if y'all can't wade the storm we in this moment then the next wave that hit us gon feel like a hurricane." Uncle Majesty said. He was a practical man, but our emotions were all over the place. His words were incomprehensible at that moment. I wasn't trying to hear no speech. I was scared. I was angry. I was questioning everything around me. At the same time I knew Unc was right. There was more pressure to come, and we couldn't be weary for long. Honestly though, I wasn't counting on anybody to step up in my father's place. Golden was still a child. Just fresh outta high school. Jasmine was turning into a basket case right before my eyes, and SJ was simply unfit. I was the chosen one. Pops had conditioned me. He'd been my mentor the whole way through. The curriculum wasn't written, but he had embedded it in my mind. I was ready. I was ready to kill and die. I was ready to destroy and rebuild. Even if it meant cutting off some blood kin, and shedding the skin I was used to.

"Twas grace that taught my heart to fear, and grace my fears relieved. How precious did that grace appear the hour I first believed"

A lady with a big angelic voice sang Amazing Grace at my father's procession. Her silky blond wig and bright red lips reminded me of an old school R&B chick. She shed tears and waved her hand to the sky. Repeating *glory glory* after every note.

When a formation of doves soared to the sky in a perfect cross, I stretched out my arms to exalt the Massive One we call God. That was nothing short of a sign that God will rise through it all. My father's untimely death wasn't in vain, and justice would prevail. I smiled a tearful smile and squeezed Golden's hand. I had to be his backbone from there on out. God bless Jasmine, but I wasn't taking any prisoners. Let the dead weight fall by the wayside. My father's casket was lowered six feet under. I watered the soil with my tears.

You know they say dreams have meanings and the more vivid dreams that last even after you've woken up are the ones that manifest in reality. My dreams were like omens preparing me for one moment to the next. Something eerie was in the air. Something wasn't right and I was beginning to question everybody around me. I kept Golden close to me, banned him from video games, pushed him to get out of the house more, kept tabs on his whereabouts. I took his pain and carried it with me like borrowed luggage.

Chapter III

Pop's lawyer Rodney Mayfield arrived at our estate on an early Wednesday afternoon. I could tell by his blue Ralph Lauren polo shirt and his Ralph Lauren khakis that it was a casual day for him. He confirmed by excitedly telling us about an amateur golf tournament he was on his way to after our briefing. Uncle Majesty had the chef cook us up a nice little brunch. Country fried steak, cheese scrambled eggs, grits, you know the whole shabang.

I noticed SJ was the perkiest I've seen him in a while. No pun intended. It took a lot for me not to blast his punk ass, but I took it for what it was. Our father had worked hard to make sure his children were A1 straight when he left this earth, so we all knew there was something major for all of us left in his will. Rodney wasted no time.

"Let's get straight to it, shall we?"

We all sat alert. Silent. My mouth watered at the delicious smelling food before me. Rodney Read each individual lasting word my father left us in his will:

"To my most honorable worldly accomplishments,
  There is no way I could have prepared any of you for this day. I myself have lived and relived the fantasy of my demise since the beginning of my thirties. Needless to say I have long awaited this day and I am fully prepared for whatever the afterlife brings or lacks. Although I know you all are saddened and consider this old man a loss, I present you with this treasure of foundation and continued legacy with hopes that you will one day do the same for the fruit of your flesh."

"Golden, my sweet baby boy. I give to you $20,000,000.00 that you are not entitled to until the day you receive your doctorate degree. My expectations for you are magnificent because I know the mighty potential you hold within. So fix your lip boy, and hold up your head. You'll be a doctor before the age twenty-seven. That is my prophecy, and so far your path has shown me that God agrees with my expectations of you, sweet baby boy.
Forever, Pops."

"Empress, my one and only daughter. My dream come true. I entrust with you my entire estate. You have shown me the utmost loyalty. You've been my best friend, my guardian angel, and my biggest supporter. God blessed me with a pure and clean heart in the form of you. Thank you young queen. I can now rest knowing that you will be shrewd, intellectual, dignified, and compassionate for my namesake.
Blessings,
Forever Pops"

Sir Jr., my first born. The greatest battle on this earth I fought was with myself for never having the

heart to give up on you. You were selfish and unreasonable with me no matter how great of an effort I made to prove my love to you. I give you nothing, because there is nothing that I could ever give you that will make you appreciate the love I have for you. Through your ungratefulness and greed you've become your own worst enemy. Blame yourself. By the time you get this you'll probably be the blame for my demise. God bless your poor heart, my foolish son.
Sadly,
Forever Pops,

Welp. It goes without saying. The smile on SJ's face was more scrambled than those cheesy eggs the chef had prepared for us. But my tears were happy ones. Pops had given selflessly to SJ's inconsiderate-ungrateful behind only to be disrespected and hated in the end. SJ didn't love Pops. He loved money. Money that he hadn't worked towards. SJ was really a spoiled brat turned studio gangster, but through it all Pops stayed solid and treated him with love and compassion. But I must say. Mane must I say. Pop's played his hand perfectly in the grand scheme of this life of spades. That Big Joker trumps all the cards in the deck.
SJ went psychotic throwing food, roaring like a fucking grizzly bear. Uncle Majesty escorted him

out to the back. Pops had left Jasmine ten million dollars, sealed with a sweet goodbye. I think that broke her more, which made me want to protect her more. Because I'd come to the realization that Jasmine truly loved my father, which was something she and I had in common. She was a broken gem that I would help nurse back to life which would take a whole lot of support and even more patience.

It took one last bad dream for me to get the entire picture. Something was looming in the air. At first I was scared. I didn't want to believe that it had come to what it'd come to, but still somehow I'd always known it would. There was a lump in my heart the weight of an elephant. But the thing about courage is you could be the most terrified you have ever been in your life, and despite your fear you face the road ahead. No matter its complexity. So yea my college educated ass was about to get some street justice for my father's life. I should have suspected him all along. Flashes of his disloyalty played over and over in my mind like a bitter slideshow. The thing about karma is that it seems like bliss on the perceiving end, because a vengeful mind is blind. But the Most High is a mysterious being. All along SJ was suffering. Deteriorating by his own guilt. SJ had many reasons to feel guilty. A deadbeat father.

A selfish brother and son. A shameless man who held no accountability for his actions. The Lean, the liquor, the coke, the pills, and all the toxic traits that came along with his downward spiral lifestyle was unmasking the demons that lived inside of him. SJ had run out of lives. I was at his neck like a razor to a chin. It was two days before the news broke publicly. I hadn't felt like myself in weeks. Cigars and gun smoke. I was doing a lot of target practice and a lot of smoking. God knows I wanted all the smoke.

Black on Black Crime : Sir Black Gunned Down by His Eldest Son

Black Supremacy Reaches an All Time Low: Media Mogul fatally shot by Son

Black Cracks After All: Sir Black Senior Murdered by Oldest Son

The Bad Black Seed: Black Supremacy founder murdered by own son

Every Media platform competed for the corniest headlines. The play on words and the mockery of my last name gave me the last little fuel I needed to blackout and bring my father his justice. I read every story. Watched every news coverage on my father's murder. SJ's photos were everywhere it seemed, but he'd remained on the run. I prayed obsessively that the police didn't catch up to him before I did. SJ knew. He knew my father had a hole in his heart. My father suffered heart ailments from a young age. He'd survived boxing, a lengthy run in the streets, and even some emotional heartache, but it was just no way he could sustain a bullet through his heart. SJ was on my hit list. A prison sentence did not weigh up to the lethal injection he had coming for him and that's on period.

Alas, nothing happened the way I'd expected. Uncle Majesty was ten steps ahead of it all. He'd tracked SJ and convinced him to turn himself in. SJ was driven safely to the precinct without so much as a scratch to show for. I was livid. It wasn't fair. Uncle Majesty was playing captain saver as if he would obtain some kinda trophy for his good deed. I vomited two days worth of meals on the family room floor. The sight of Uncle Majesty hugging SJ's neck and kissing his cheek made me sick to my stomach. Betrayal at its finest. My father's murderer didn't deserve sympathy or pity. He deserved hate and public shame. There was my father's supposed to be brother embracing his killer like a precious son. That sealed the lid closed for me. Uncle Majesty was in on my father's murder. I couldn't unsee it. Why else would he carefully protect SJ?

My father had an upscale office deep off in the cut of Downtown Memphis. It was his private office. The location was unknown to most. Uncle Majesty was very familiar with the office since he handled some of my father's most personal business. I waited in the dark office for nearly twelve hours. At my father's desk, I sat orchestrating the outcome of the scenario I created in my mind. My levels of wickedness and thirstiness for blood had skyrocketed. I was restless and unpredictable. When he finally entered the office, I cocked the pistol three times like I was Candyman or something. I heard his pistol cock at the third time I cocked mine. I spun around in the chair and fired an intentional bullet through the door just inches away from his temple. He ducked to the floor, scrambling to locate the light switch. When the light turned on I was standing with my back turned as I watched the Memphis horizon through the enormous 20th floor window. He shifted the weight of his foot. I could feel him burning a hole through me with his one good eye.

"Empress?" "Are you out of your goddamn mind?"

"Why?"

"Why what?" What are you asking me?"

"A sucker took out a king and you helped him. How does it feel to be Judas to a man who would have given you his right arm if you asked him to?"

"Empress, what are you saying to me?"

"My daddy's gone and that piece of shit disgrace of a man gets to live."

Uncle Majesty eased toward me with caution. "C'mon niece. You know me better than that. This thing we live is a game of chess not checkers, baby girl."

"Prison is not enough for what he's done."

"Don't you think I know that, Empress?" "Or did you expect me to put a bullet in his brain for the whole world to see?"

I turned to face him. He placed his pistol on the desk despite the fact that I still had my finger on the trigger.

"Empress don't get me wrong, I understand how this all might look to you. Not knowing who to trust or whose a suspect. But I am a man first and I am my brother's keeper second. Never question my loyalty to my brother. Even in his death I am indebted to the oath we made between each other." Uncle Majesty said.

I could see him holding back tears. Wise men act on patience and precise actions, while young ambitious ones like myself acted on emotions and raw impulse. I needed that instant pleasure of knowing SJ wouldn't see another peaceful night. Uncle Majesty went on to explain his reasoning behind the peaceful exchange while turning SJ over to the Memphis police department.

"They'd never suspect a loyal, loving, and honorable uncle. They'll never see me coming." He said.

"I want in. I won't sleep until he feels my wrath." I said.

40

Uncle Majesty gave me a funny look but he didn't object. I made it clear that I wasn't seeking permission. I would handle it with or without him.

Of course SJ never saw it coming. In his twisted mind he'd become an infamous legend. Accepting interviews and even signing on for book deals and documentaries. The boost in music streams and youtube views validated his ignorant conceit. He had become so full of himself that he never expected judgment day was upon him. Uncle Majesty was married to a highly intelligent pediatrician from up north. She'd done her doctoral thesis on the science of vaccines and lethal injections. She'd informed uncle Majesty, upon his request, of an injection that had a poison that turns organs to stone in a matter of sixteen hours. Uncle Majesty had gotten hold of the formula via an anonymous source.

I needed to see him. I needed to speak with him, before he met his final fate. There was so much I had to say, but when we were finally face to face. I turned cold and still as stone. SJ showed no remorse. He entered the visitation room with an arrogant smile. His head held high like the world was his and the rest of us were just his bitches. When we locked eyes his eyes turned evil but his smile stayed. I always knew SJ had it in him. Only a coward triumphs in travesty. I sat unprovoked. Searching his eyes. I spotted the coward within and he cracked beneath my gaze. SJ had not succeeded. He was a dead man walking and didn't know it. He had not obtained any real success. I was the holder of my father's estate. I was the mogul, I had become king. He was left taking scraps from my daddy's name. Silly fool! I read him like the fictional book he was. All fiction. No facts. This nigga was pathetic.

"What are you doing here?" SJ asked.

I stared harshly at him. I could have spat in his face. My heart began to race, but a cold air grazed over and made me calm. So I sat breathing and listening to my heartbeat. I had nothing left to say to SJ, he was worthless. He was finished. I owed him nothing, and he had nothing to give. Justice had come, and I had come out on top through all of it.

"I came to say my last goodbye." I said.

SJ frowned, then squinted his eyes. He rolled his shoulders forward, resting on his elbows. Saying, "Keep your goodbye, you dead to me. All of y'all."

He yelled for the guard and was guided back onto the cellblock.

7a.m. the next day, the news announced SJ dead. His cause of death was unknown. The prison officials suspected suicide, overdoes, or something like that. I shut off the television and rested like an angel.

My father came to me in my dream. He was on an island. It was paradise. The sky was pink and peachy. The sun sat on the calm sea. The weather was perfect. It smelled like mangoes and coconut. He exited his bungalow with two cigars in his head. A wide happy smile and arms spreaded out to hug. I ran into his embrace.

"Pop, I missed you." I said.

"I know daughter, but I knew we'd meet again. I'm so proud of you. You're a different woman now. You've overcome the unthinkable. I can rest now, knowing that everything's covered."

"Yes Sir, you can rest up. I got it from here Pops." I always got us."

TRIPPIN' LIKE A MF

By

Damita Taylor

Mecca took her last shot from a fifth of henny. Squinting her watery eyes upward at the beaming sun. The sadness of talking to her granny through the dirt weighed heavy on her heart and mind. It'd been four years since her granny passed, but somehow the sadness revealed itself in the least expected of times. She had gotten so used to hiding her true emotion that even though she was alone she fought her tears from falling. She tried to breathe through it, the cool air she inhaled helped her make it to the car. Her black on black Nissan was a hefty downgrade from her Benz truck. Her last lover Woo took her through a phase of enlightenment and caused her to give up most of her luxuries. No more flashy jewelry aside from the iced out pendant of her beloved grandmother. She went from rocking designer clothes to only rocking styles she invented from her own sewing machine and printer press. Mecca's creative mind had placed her in a position to do excellent for herself financially, but these days she was just stacking money with no intentions to splurge or flex. Live humble and prosper was her life's motto.

She sped off from the cemetery in a rush to make it to her first therapy session. Jhene Aiko' W. A.Y.S played at high volume from her car's bluetooth.

Jhene' sweet soulful voice helped her through every mood. She ended up on the south side of memphis. The therapist office was a modern house. The sign in the front yard read, Zillion Moor House of Therapy. A garden in the front yard, the scent of fresh grown tomatoes and leafy greens glided through her nostrils and overpowered the otherwise odorous presence of pollution. Mecca went to knock on the door, but was stopped in her tracks by a voice projected through an intercom:

"Mecca Ali, I am glad to have you. I was afraid you wouldn't show up, girl. Come in. Walk straight through I'll be in the last room on your right." Zillion greeted her.

Mecca was instantly intrigued, but far from impressed. What type of therapist was this? Was she one of those social media gurus who got more of a kick out of the appearance of healing than actual healing? Was she the type to expose her clients for clicks and views? Some lame ass writer using her clients' stories to make money from cheesy ass self help books? Hmm.. Mecca wondered, and would soon find out.
The home was like a mini enchanted forest. Plants were everywhere, all types of plants. The hardwood floors were made of tree bark. The floors didn't

creak when she walked on them, it was silent, still, solid. Mecca was lit and on edge from the henny vibes, but a calming sensation came over her as she walked farther into the house.

Dr. Zillion Moor sat in her velvet pink wooden leg chair. A sweet aroma totally relaxed Mecca to the point that she slouched down in one of the comfy client chairs before Zillion offered her a seat.

"I would say cheers to Happy Hour but all the bars are closed. Social distancing is a vacay for some and solitary confinement for others." Zillion said and cracked a smile at her own sarcasm.

"It's neither for me." Mecca replied straight-faced.

"I'm sorry that I offended you by my assumption."Zillion said.

"Nah you good, you good. I'm drunker than a mothafucka, but I ain't been on a vacay or shit like that." Mecca said.

"Where have you been, Mecca? If you don't mind me asking?" Zillion asked.

"I went to visit my granny's grave." Mecca replied.

"Oh I see, how did that work out for you?"

"Talking to that dirt instead of her face just makes me miss her even more."

"That's unfortunate. How long has it been since she passed?"

"Four years."

" Were you two close?"

"That lady was my whole world."

"Powerful. How has her absence affected your day to day?"

"My whole world flipped upside down. I know she would be proud of how far I came but I'll give all this up to have her back."

"I'm sure she'd be very proud." Zillion said, then she crossed her legs and asked, " Do you want to die, Mecca?"

Mecca pondered the question intensely. Though it came from left field. She understood that it was a clean up way to ask have she ever considered

48

suicide. Mecca felt like she was dying on multiple occasions, but she didn't want to die. She wanted to feel better. She wanted the life she once loved back. Mecca shook her head, replying "Nah, I wanna live."

"Okay, then. That's a good start." Zillion said, giving Mecca an assuring smile.

They were quiet for a moment. Taking in each other's auras. Filling the energy of the room. Mecca. Zillion had observed, was a cool one. From her newly growing locs to her makeshift navy blue short sleeve button up with the jean shorts to match. Mecca's aura was masculine and magnetic. She hadn't smiled but Zillion peeped the gold studded diamond on her teeth. Mecca's skin was brown and smooth like maple syrup. Zillion cleared her throat, finding herself getting wrapped in Mecca's beauty. Mecca watched Zillion right back, she observed her right back. Yes, Zillion was fine, slim-thick, skin smooth like a bowl of dark chocolate. But all women were on Mecca's shit list thanks to Woo, her last lover. Pussy didn't excite her like it used to. What used to be her deepest desire now bored her. She'd been hurt by one woman too many, a woman she loved profoundly. Now she was left to recoup and start from a clean slate.

Mecca stared piercingly at Zillion. "You don't look a day over twenty-two. How old are you?" She asked.

Zillion shifted, slightly uneased by Mecca's question, but slightly flattered.

Zillion smiled. "I'm thirty years old. You don't look a day over twenty yourself." She said.

"I'm twenty-eight. But aye I actually like your energy. I was iffy about this therapy shit at first, but I think we're off to a good start too. " Mecca said.

"What convinced you to come here? Or should I ask who convinced you to come here?" Zillion asked.

"My home girl told me this would be good for me." Mecca replied.

Zillion nodded and smiled. She knew Mecca was holding back. Mecca showed symptoms of heart break. The loss of her granny wasn't recent enough. Mecca was grieving a new loss. She was like an open wound sitting on the therapy couch. Zillion could see straight through the cool fasade, and the nonchalant attitude. Mecca was vulnerable, and Zillion wouldn't be the expert she was if she hadn't pushed the envelope just a little, in order to get Mecca to open up.

"Your eyes are so sad, Mecca. What's bothering you?" Zillion asked.

Mecca was silent. She knew Zillion was reading her and could probably see straight through her. Alas, it was Zillion's job to read body languages and minds, damn near. Mecca was uncomfortable. She was unable to express the root of her pain. Zillion leaned forward and patted Mecca' knee with an encouraging smile.

"What's bothering you, Mecca?" Zillion asked again.

"I can't call it. I'm not used to this feeling. All I know is I want it to go away." Mecca finally, replied. The watery eyes returned, but she blinked them away. No tears fell from her eyes, still Zillion offered Mecca the box of tissues.

"This is a safe space, it's okay to let go." Zillion said, her voice was soft and encouraging.

Mecca took a couple tissues, but she wasn't ready to cry, not yet. Zillion saw Mecca's pain was deep rooted, far greater than even Mecca herself thought it was. She knew she had what she liked to call hardcore lightwork on her hands.

"Mecca sweety I have a question, that I'm not sure you're comfortable enough to answer." Zillion said then watched for Mecca's reaction to her words.

"I have nothing to lose. Shoot your best shot."Mecca said and her words trailed off."...The world ain't been shit since my granny left it." Mecca said, in a daze. Her voice trembled, her lips quivered.

Again, Mecca found herself holding back the water that wanted to fall from her eyes. She wouldn't even need a therapist if her granny was alive. Her granny was her rock and always knew just what to say to get Mecca back on track. She massaged her temples, staring down at the floor with a mask of confusion and dizziness. She shook her head sluggishly and made it to the small trash can in just the knick of time, vomiting ferociously. Zillion rolled her eyes, left the room, only to return with a cup of water and a washcloth. Mecca sat on the floor hugging the trash can. Zillion wiped Mecca's face with the washcloth. The warmth of the cloth soothed Mecca. The water was room temperature. Mecca could tell by the taste that it was spring water. She dropped the cup of water and vomited some more. Zillion knew Mecca had probably drunk more than her share of liquor, but still she consoled her without judgment.

"Who hurt you, Mecca?" Zillion asked.

"Nobody." Mecca replied.

Mecca frowned with confusion. Zillion really could see straight through her. Still Mecca lied. Zillion knew it was a lie, because she answered too quickly. She was right, Mecca wasn't comfortable enough yet.

Mecca left Zillion's office feeling as vulnerable as an open wound. Her thoughts were interrupted by Tonya's call on her car's bluetooth. Jumping right into it, Tonya asked ,"How was it bitch? Your bullheaded ass didn't give my girl Z a hard time did you?"

Mecca smirked, "It was cool. I like her."

"Whaaat!" I did that huh. I know you like a book, Mecca. I knew y'all would have that dope ass chemistry."

Mecca shook her head. "Aw I see, that big ass head of yours must be about to explode, how you gas'n yaself right now." Mecca said, trying to humble Tonya just a little bit.

Tonya giggled. "Okay friend, okay. I get your lil' hint. But know this, I know you. And I'm happy that I know you. I thank God everyday for that and I would go crazy if I lose you. That's why I'm so stoked that you like Z. She's amazing at what she does, I trust her with you." She said.

Mecca smiled wide and bright. " Yes ma'am, one ah dem." She replied. Tonya laughed. Her friend was so laid back, and nonchalant that it was simply comical to her, but she knew what Mecca meant. Mecca showed love effortlessly, and she spoke it in her own way.

"So what's the move?" Mecca asked. She was in the mood for a much needed turn up. Something lowkey though. If anybody could make that a success it was Tonya.

" Knowing you, it's something with Henny involved, and I know you trying to come up tonight, so one of your little sneaky linkies most definitely on the invite list."

"Yea one ah dem, that's a bet, tacos too, put shrimp tacos on the menu, friend."

Tonya laughed. "Girl, say less. I'm already on it. I'll be round your way no later than 7pm."

Mecca ended the call smiling. Jhene Aiko Pussy Fairy resumed playing on her car bluetooth.

***

Eight o' clock in the evening. Zillion turns into the cove of her residence, Her stomach instantly growls. She'd intermittent fasted for twelve hours, and now her mouth watered for some top notch smoked salmon, made from scratch macaroni and cheese, cornbread muffins, and candied yams that she would wash down with a chilled glass of blackberry- lemon tea.

"Zion your momma's home." Zeal, Zillion's mother yelled from the kitchen.

"Hey to you too momma." Zillion said. Kissing Zeal's face.

"Oh baby, you know I'm glad you home, go tell that child of yours to put that phone away so we can have supper." Zeal said, kissing her face to Zillion's as she made the plates.

"You a fool nigga, tried to rob me and got popped. That's on my tool nigga. Once I get to tweakin ain't no stoppin me..." Zillion heard Zion rapping Sir Tha Savage lyrics. Zillion was concerned by her daughter's obsession with a rapper who was well known for murdering his own father, but Zillion was fine with her listening to him through her personal airpods.

Zillion walked in on her daughter twerking in the mirror, wearing nothing but boy shorts and a Nike sports bra. It still left Zillion dumbfounded that she had a sixteen year old daughter. Zion had gone from a sweet colorful barrettes wearing girl to a sassy trap music loving hot girl. Zillion knew it was just a phase, but she was not impressed by what she'd started to see in her child. Zion stopped dancing as soon as she saw Zillion in her mirror. Zillion ignored the shocked expression on Zion's face. Instead she removed the airpods from her ear one by one.

Zillion softly pinched her cheek, watching her with so much wonder and compassion. It was so hard to believe that this soon to be woman had come from her vagina. Zion looked slightly embarrassed.

"Momma you gotta knock before you come in here. I'm not a little child anymore. I need my privacy." She said.

Zillion smirked, "Girl having a closed door in a house that you pay nothing for is privacy enough. You wanna have a door that I have to knock before I enter, then you need to be getting your own house."

Zion just rolled her eyes, tilted her neck and stared at her. Zillion rubbed her hand through Zion's long passion twists.

"Dinner is ready, and I'm starving. Come on." Zillion said.

Zion came down stairs in a Cash Money records graphic tee and colorful leggings.

"Well isn't it about time, seems like the only time I see your butt is when you ready to either work my nerves or your greedy self looking for something to eat." Zeal said, poking fun at her granddaughter.

Zion smacked her lips, and grasped her shoulder, feeling betrayed. "Granny stop showing out we played best out of ten on UNO today, and I watched Divorce Court with you."

"I know baby, we be chillin. I just like messing with you."

"Uh huh, where does school work fit into all this chilling y'all been doing?"

"Momma relax, I'm all the way caught up on my school work. My teachers told me I could chill."

"Um hm, baby are you going to bless the food?"

"Sure momma. Dear infinite most powerful source, we thank you for the meal you have provided for us through your gift of abundance and life. May this meal nourish our mind, bodies, and spirits, so that we may better serve you. Ase`." Zillion prayed. She opened her eyes to find her mother staring dumbfoundedly at her, mouth wide open.

"What is it ma?"

"Nothing. I'm just gon' keep my thoughts to myself. But you know I'm used to praying in the name of Jesus."

Zion and Zillion shared a look and both began cracking up. Zeal dug her fork into her macaroni and turned up her lips. "Everybody got they own preference on how to talk to'em I guess." She said under her breath.

"C'mon Granny, How you mad at momma cause she prayed different from how you pray?" Zion asked while cracking up. "

"I'm saying." Zillion said, chiming in.

"How yall like the mac and cheese. I think I could have left it in the oven a few minutes longer." Zeal said, avoiding the question. She knew she had no real argument up against her daughters. They were three generations of women at one table. They all were raised in three different eras. So Zeal understood her daughter's beliefs, values, and traditions would be completely different from her own. Sometimes she just got beside herself, because the way she was raised meant the mother had all the say so. And who momma praised that's who the children praised. But alas, times were different and the youth had learned different ways to worship and communicate with God. They called it being spiritual and not religious, even though Zeal was wondering what in the hell was the difference.

While Zillion showered, and Zeal did Gospel Zumba downstairs in the family room. Zion was texting a boy named Shamir, who she met at a rival school's basketball game before the Quarantine fell in effect. He was two years older, curly hair with swag and a crazy shoe game. Zion had been following his Snapchat and instagram, and saw that he was a popular dude with a budding rap and youtube career. Girls from all over wanted him, but he was coming so hard for her. She liked that they had things in common. He was raised by women and he was a good big brother to his younger siblings. They bonded mostly over music and having a few mutual friends. They had just agreed to facetime each other, when Zillion entered Zion's room. Zillion wore a bathrobe and had her head wrapped in a towel. She sat on the bed next to Zion.

"I was two years younger than you when I gave birth to you. Did you know that?" Zillion asked. Zion shifted nervously, but remained silent. Understanding that her momma must have been going somewhere with her statement. Mother's intuition was so real. Any woman who claims to not know if her child is going through something or hiding something was a flat out liar. A mother knows. Zillion could sense when something was off about her daughter. She also understood that multiple things could be the result of her child's changed behavior. Especially her new interest in boys and possibly sex. They were both silent. Filling out each other's energy. There was no need to rush through the conversation. Their hearts would reveal what needed to be said in the right moment.

"Yeah, grandma told me."Zion said, then hung her head thoughtfully.

"Yea she was really disappointed in me when she first found out." Zillion said, she bit her lip. The memory still stung even though she and her mother had moved far past that.

"Momma, I don't ever want to disappoint you, but I'm just a kid. I'm not perfect. I'm going to mess up. I might mess up really bad, because I'm still learning, but can we make a promise?"

"What's that babe?" Zillion asked.

"Promise you won't ever stop loving me no matter what."Zion pleaded.

"I promise, baby. I love you and all your imperfections. There's nothing you could do to ever make me stop loving you no matter how upset and disappointed you may make me." Zillion pledged.

Zion exhaled. A weight had been lifted off of her. "I'm your only child, girl. We stuck together remember that." Zion said.

Zillion twisted her nose and turned her mouth sideways, then she nudged Zion playfully. Truth be told, they had a special relationship. Zillion was fourteen years old when she gave birth to Zion. Zillion raised Zion with the help of her mother and late father. Zion's daddy was sent away six months after her birth for a double homicide and aggravated robbery. Zillion, like many good girls, had fallen for a street dude, and it nearly threatened her own freedom. Zeal and Teddy were two loving parents who fought undyingly for the betterment and safety of their one and only daughter. They compromised and sacrificed so much to protect her. They picked up a lot of her slack and forgave many of her foolish mistakes. Zillion was living proof of what a mother and father's unconditional love and devotion could do. She wanted to represent that kind of love for Zion. Zion and Zillion were mother and daughter, but they also had a sisterly bond.

"I want you to come to my office tomorrow. I got something I want to show you." Zillion said.

"Okay that's cool with me, momma,"

"Good. Get you some rest. Shut that phone off, it's not good for your sleep regulation."

Zion rolled her eyes. "You doing too much now." Zion said.

Zillion pinched her nose. "Do as I say little girl."

Zion nodded reluctantly. Like all teenagers she was hardheaded, but she would eventually do as her mother said, after her facetime call with Shamir that is. Zillion kissed Zion's face and headed for the door, when Zion said something that stopped her.

"Momma I got a boyfriend." She said and a look of terror snuck upon her face.

Zillion watched her from over her shoulder a few seconds too long. "I figured you did, but I'm happy

63

you finally told me. We'll talk more about him tomorrow. Shut that phone off." Zillion replied. Yep, it was time for her to officially take Zion under her wing. An idle mind leaves too much open space for the devil to play.

****

Tonya had made good on her word. She came through with the tacos, liquor, a couple real ones, and two baddies for Mecca to choose from. Everybody was lowkey drunk. Laid back chilling in Mecca's living room, playing a game of Never Have I Ever. Kiana, one of the baddies, decided to test the waters with Mecca by asking a provocative question.

"So Mecca, answer me this. Have you ever had penis envy?"

"First of all Kiana, what the fuck do that shit mean?"Mecca asked.

From the opposite couch Tonya and her girlfriend, Zay, instigated. "Oh shit, it's starting to get real grown and messy in here." Tonya said, being playful. Attentively, Zay leaned forward, and Tonya wrapped both arms around Zay's tattooed sleeve.

Kiana grinned a mischievous smile, it was obvious that she was seeking a way to get under Mecca's skin. "It means have you ever envied a man because he has a real dick and you don't?"

Mecca leaned back. Her golds sparkled as she licked her lips and frowned. "Pussy and dick don't compete. Most of my bitches like pussy, they don't fuck with dick, don't even want me to strap'em." Mecca said.

Kiana was intrigued. "So how do you please them if you don't strap'em?"

Mecca smiled. She had Kiana right where she liked them, curious and open like a book. "That's for me to know and for you to find out." Mecca said.

Kiana lowered her eyes and shrugged her shoulders. "Um well I wasn't really seeking, I was just making conversation." She said and sipped her short glass of henny.

Mecca didn't let up on her. A heat grew between Kiana' thighs as she watched Mecca undress her with her eyes. Kiana was on the hood side, but she had a fierce shape that women would literally die for. Succulent lips dazzled with lush lip gloss. She fiddled with the Blonde bangs that covered her forehead. Mecca had noticed earlier in the night that she wasn't wearing panties under her red, pink, and black floral mini dress. She had an enticing voice with a southern twang, and she had a certain toughness about her that Mecca admired. Kiana was definitely on Mecca's late night early morning hit list.

The tension between them was felt throughout the room. Brittnay the other girl Tonya had invited was salty at not being the subject of Mecca's attention, but Zay's friend Dee alley hooped that pass and made sure to put a smile on Brittnay's face before the night was over. Mecca's home was spacious and comfy. She had a master's bedroom with two guest rooms, and a lair that would make any bachelor proud.

Each couple retired to their own private area of the house. Mecca and Kiana chilled out in Mecca's lair. Mecca wanted Kiana wide open and slightly on edge. Mecca had a LED light and motion projector installed that acted as a travelling telescope the way it displayed a slideshow of all the planets, moon phases, stars, and galaxies across the ceiling. Under usual circumstances, Mecca would play her turn-a-bitch-out playlist, but tonight she took a different approach. She let the vibe between them speak for itself.

They sat on the lion skin rug. Their backs against the cushiony velvet blue lounge sofa. Facing the built-in seventy inch aquarium. Mecca began strumming Kiana' thigh like her personal guitar.

"I can tell you never did this before." Mecca said. Kiana nodded nervously.

"It's a first time for everything, though." She shyly shrugged.

Mecca leaned in close enough for their lips to touch then said, "Seems like you ready for me."

Kiana smiled, rolled her eyes. "Girl you a trip." She said.

They were spinning off the liquor. Mecca french kissed Kiana' neck. Kiana bit her lip with satisfaction. There was the difference, the passion, the subtlety of a woman's tongue exploring her body. Kiana' eyes nearly popped out of the sockets when Mecca came out of her white tee and black loose-fitted Land of Trill shorts. Her body looked fierce in her Ralph Lauren sports bra and boxer briefs. Mecca smiled, then helped Kiana come out of her dress. Kiana had pierced nipples and a belly ring. Mecca had fun with that. Mixing pain and pleasure, she bit Kiana' nipples then twirled her tongue around her piercings. Kiana moaned. Rubbing her fingers through Mecca's hair. Mecca straddled Kiana' lap and grinded slowly. Kiana thrusted and grinded back. Mecca stopped grinding. "One ah dem, give me that pussy." Mecca entered two fingers inside of Kiana' warm-wetness, and moved them as if he was playing the piano and slow dancing with her fingers. It was the mental enticement, more than the sex itself that had Kiana' mind gone. She was open to all the touchy feely moves Mecca had up her sleeves. Mecca took her time with Kiana. She turned Kiana on her stomach and began licking and sucking Kiana' neck and spine. She made Kiana toot her cakes in the air and fingered her from the back. Mecca knew what Kiana really wanted, but she let the anticipation build first. She smacked Kiana' cakes. Kiana arched her back more and opened her legs wider. Mecca began thrusting into Kiana hard and slow. Kiana hummed and moaned. Mecca was having fun. It was total mind fuck for Kiana and she knew it. Her ego was stroked, so there was nothing left to do but give the woman what she so desperately wanted. Mecca ate her out from the back like a bowl of peaches and cream. Mecca lost count of how many times she made Kiana cum. All she knew was before the sun came up Kiana was cuddled into her arms like they were married.

Hours later, Mecca awoke with a heavy heart and a mind full of sad bitter thoughts. She hopped straight into a cold shower because the discomfort of the shivering coldness pouring onto her skin made her feel alive and in the moment. That was how she started each and everyday otherwise she'd lay paralyzed by the endless pain that swallowed her whole. She'd finally noticed the smell of warm waffles, fruit, and smoked meat. She remembered the night before, and she'd finally remembered Kiana. For a moment, when the pain was too great, and her heart would not allow her to feel, see, hear, smell, or taste, all she managed to do was walk and breathe. But she had returned to reality. She could function again, yet and still, the pain stayed. The pain she couldn't escape, neither could she diagnose its root cause.

"It's about time you joined us, sleepy head." Tonya said to Mecca who stood in the doorway.

There on her outdoor patio eating breakfast, sat Kiana and Brittnay, Dee, Tonya and Zay. Kiana checked out Mecca then smiled. Mecca grabbed a seat opposite of her and grabbed two waffles from the platter. Kiana kept staring, seductively she licked her lips. Mecca ignored her flirty gestures. Kiana shrugged.

"I see what type of time we on." Kiana said, chuckling. She kept right along eating once she realized Mecca was paying her no mind. Everyone acted as if the awkward tension didn't exist. They kept eating while keeping the topic on another subject.

"Niggas really out here acting foolish with these stimulus checks." Zay said reading a social media post off her phone.

"Fools really buying out electronics and tissue when they really need to be stacking that lil check and making sure they be straight when shit blow over." Zay said. Tonya and the others agreed.

" I just invested mines. Let that shit work for me while I sleep." Tonya said.

"Good for you but everybody don't know how to invest." Kiana said.

"Nah see it's not about whether they know how to invest or not. You gotta be interested in learning to invest and most folks just ain't interested." Tonya said.

"I'm interested, I just don't know how." Kiana said.

"Well what are you doing to learn how?" Tonya asked.

Kiana didn't reply. Mecca was quiet. She could tell Kiana craved her attention, but Mecca wanted her to disappear. Kiana was attached to a memory Mecca needed to forget. Mecca was beginning to feel shame in her budding addiction to Hennessy and hoes. These chicks weren't supposed to rise and shine and break bread with Mecca and her close friends. They were supposed to get their cheeks clapped and dash. In Mecca's eyes Kiana and Brittany had overstayed their welcome, and that turned her off.

"Aye what time is it?" Mecca asked, annoyed and over the fakeness.

"It's nine a.m." Tonya replied.

" Bet. Y'all gotta be out by nine-thirty cause I got somewhere to be." Mecca said.

Tonya peeped Mecca's vibe and followed suit. "Ah man I almost forgot about that lil play we chopped about the other day. Bae gotta be at work by ten a.m. anyway. Right bae?" Tonya said, nudging Zay as a cue to go along.

"That's a bet." Zay said.

"Say less." Kiana said. "We out then Britt, let's roll." She said.

Mecca couldn't help but watch the extra twist in Kiana's hips as she walked away. Dee left with Kiana and Brittany. That left Tonya and Zay. Tonya's attitude switched fast.

"Damn Mecca. You are so hard on these bitches I feel bad for them sometimes. I don't see how you fuck a girl like you love her when you know you don't care nothing about her." Tonya said.

"That's a dangerous game." Zay said.

"I serve them up. I don't force shit. I just give them what they want then after that I'm done." Mecca said.

"Friend you better than that. You need to be mindful of how you act on certain shit. You might be hurting somebody who really means you well." Tonya said.

"I'm not trying to hurt nobody, I aim to please. Everything after that is self inflicted. If a chick think we gone fall in love and live a happy ever after based off some good sex that's on her stupid ass." Mecca said.

"Ever since Woo left you, something been off about you. I can't put my finger on it. But sometimes I don't know who you are. I mean like I for real can't recognize you." Tonya said.

Mecca was triggered by Tonya' statement, but she shrugged it off. " I am who I am. Take it or leave it." She said.

"Nah this ain't the Mecca I know. This here is some cold hearted wanna-be pretender using Mecca's body." Tonya said.

73

Mecca felt a way about Tonya's words. However, Mecca knew Tonya was right. Mecca became a stranger to herself too. Still, she found reason to argue.

"Maybe that mean you and me done outgrew one another." Mecca said.

"Girl, maybe so. But when you are ready to face the real lemme know." Tonya said with obvious agitation.

Tonya and Zay cleared the table, cleaned the kitchen after themselves, then dipped out.
Mecca was left in the house all alone. A nauseous feeling came to her gut and made her rush to the toilet bowl. She hugged the toilet as she threw up her entire breakfast. A sharp pain pierced her sides causing her to curl and scream. The emotional pain had turned physical. She felt like she was being attacked by an unknown entity. All Mecca could do was crumble into the fetal position and cry. She cried for help. "What is wrong with me?" She screamed. "What is wrong with me?" She whimpered. Then, the memory of a face that she'd done her damndest to forget had crept its way back into Mecca's mind. Her tears turned cold. The source of her pain was revealing itself. She was

simply in denial. Her pride wouldn't let her accept that she was that weak behind a female. A woman that vanished from her life without any clear reason. Woo, her lover of four years had picked up and left one night with no more to say than " I can't do this anymore." Mecca had been going with the motions since Woo left her. Mecca was lovesick but she was too ashamed to admit it.

   Two weeks later, Mecca sits on the therapy couch in Zillion's office. This time around Mecca was ready to be honest. She opened up about her relationship with Woo, and how it went south. Woo had come into Mecca's life at a crucially vulnerable time. It was one month after her granny passed. Mecca was on a panel at a black creatives conference in Atlanta. Woo was a guest at the conference as well, she was promoting a play that she'd written and produced. Woo instantly caught Mecca's eye. She was feminine, feisty, intelligent, and full of life. She had tattoos in all the right places, and Mecca fantasized about what she'd do if Woo ever came to her shop for a tattoo.
After the panel, Mecca and Woo mixed and mingled with others but they were sure to make their way over to each other. Mecca's first attraction was physical, but once they talked and really looked each other in the eyes it became deeper. Woo was

an Atlanta native. That was her city. Mecca was from Memphis, but had made the impulsive decision to stay in Atlanta in order to get closer to Woo. Woo was sweet to Mecca. She liked Mecca's masculine aura. Mecca was more masculine than most men. She carried herself like a king and that's what attracted Woo.

The fancy dates, designer clothes, jewelry, and spontaneous trips across the world were cool. Woo enjoyed Mecca's adventurous side. She liked nice things, but she wasn't only focused on the material things all the time. That didn't excite her as much. Woo challenged Mecca to experience new things like visiting the Buddha temple, reading new books, traveling with a purpose. She encouraged Mecca to start an art class for local youth. Woo thought Mecca had enough talent and charisma to keep the youth inspired. Mecca was versatile and accepting of Woo' suggestion. They got along great at first, then Mecca made a mistake. She cheated on Woo the second year of their relationship. Woo was heartbroken and didn't speak to Mecca for two months. Mecca attempted to get over their breakup by entertaining other women. Mecca had come to accept the distance between them, but one night out of the blue Woo called her over. They made up and made love. Mecca vowed to never betray Woo' trust again, and she didn't. But once they were together again things weren't the same. Mecca had begun doing everything Woo asked of her, but Woo was never satisfied. Although she never said it Woo' actions showed that she hadn't fully forgiven Mecca for cheating. She wasn't as sweet as she used to be. She even tried to get violent with Mecca on one occasion but Mecca wasn't the type to allow that. However Mecca respected Woo too much to let that be their way of handling conflict. Woo wanted to change Mecca into a domesticated stud wife. She tried to convince Mecca that they should find a surrogate and have a child together. Mecca loved Woo, but that wasn't the lifestyle she envisioned for herself. Woo couldn't take it. After two more years of trying to force a traditional life Woo dipped, and haven't picked up the phone for Mecca ever since.

Zillion allowed Mecca to vent her story uninterrupted. Mecca was so deep into her memory that she almost forgot Zillion was in the room. When Mecca was done reminiscing she and Zillion set in silence for several minutes. As a psychologist, Zillion understood how intense it was for someone to relive an impactful period of their life, so she wanted Mecca to soak up the energy that came along with that instead of running from it by rushing to explain her emotions. Zillion felt there was no need for an explanation, only acceptance and understanding in order for Mecca to heal from the hurt. That way she wouldn't make those same mistakes. That way she could be empowered by the lesson of the loss instead of feeling victimized. Zillion knew it was hard for someone like Mecca to show any inkling of weakness. She decided to help Mecca through those heavy emotions that came when one spoke heartily about situations they couldn't control.

"How does that make you feel?" Zillion asked.

"Like a bitch ass coward. I need to move on. No matter how hard I try not to, I still miss her." Mecca said.

"Why shouldn't you miss her?" Zillion asked.

Mecca thought it through then replied, "Because she turned her back on me when I needed her the most."

"So should you punish yourself for making good on the emotional promises you vowed to keep?" Zillion asked.

"What do you mean?" Mecca asked, confused.

"She left you without closure, so now you have unanswered questions about the love you two shared. And so naturally you would miss her and want her to return to you with answers. "Why do you feel like a coward for that?" Zillion asked.

"Because nothing lasts forever and bitches ain't shit so I should've kept my heart guarded. I slipped, and Woo took something from me and I don't know if I'll ever get it back. She won't answer my calls. She don't reply to my text. And here I am thinking about her, hoping she doing well. I'm still in love and it got me so deep in my feelings that I gotta come to therapy." Mecca answered.

"Not because you are a coward, though. Your feelings are common Mecca, but a part of you knows that you can't stay in that sunken place. You know that you must heal and move on at some point. But right now you can't do it alone, and that's why you're here. Not because you are a coward, but because you are real with yourself."

Mecca nodded. She had just experienced her first successful therapy session. With her guards down, Mecca was able to joke a little and make Zillion smile. They shook hands and enjoyed a cup of coffee together. Zillion introduced Mecca to her daughter Zion, who was multitasking in the secretarial office, messaging friends, and entering data for upcoming schedules and reports in excel spreadsheet, and watching makeup tutorials all at once. Mecca felt happy for a little while, she was glad to have someone to help her work through some of her difficult baggage.

Mecca lied awake in her bed staring at the ceiling. Woo was on her mind heavy. Woo had a smile that could sweeten the bitterest of hearts. She had a soul that could awake the dead. With just one touch, a hug, or kiss she could heal the sick. Woo was a goddess in Mecca's mind. She was everything she'd hoped for in a woman. She couldn't help but wonder if Woo thought of her the same way. She tried her luck one last time and texted Woo. Her heart pounded, hoping to get a response. She waited and waited until she fell asleep.

Then the three dots bubbled. Woo' number was saved under 'My Dream Girl 👑👑🍫🍩🍩❤'.

From My Dream Girl 👑👑🍫🍩🍩❤:
"Hey baby I'm sorry I've been neglecting you. I miss us too."

Woo messaged Mecca that sweet nothing along with a sexy photo of them together in bed. Mecca's head rested between Woo' thighs. Mecca heart raced, her breath sped up when she received the text message. The photo sent Mecca swinging back into that very moment.

"You know my body so well. That's dangerous and it doesn't sit right with me." Woo said as Mecca traced an invisible masterpiece on her inner thigh.

Mecca grinned mischievously. "You're safe with me, don't even trip."

Woo rolled her eyes. "You scare me."

"Why tho?"

"Because.."

"Because what?"

"Nah, I don't wanna say it."

"Why, you think I'm gonna hurt you or something?"

Woo nodded and pulled away from Mecca. It was a rainy day in Decatur in the late afternoon. They had just finished brunch in bed topped with a lovemaking session. Woo cradled herself under the satin sheets. Mecca almost got mad, thinking Woo was making a problem where there was none. Then she inhaled, exhaled, and leaned over to kiss Woo. She wanted to assure her that what they had was real, and that nothing real could be threatened.

"I love you girl, you my soul." Mecca said, and gave herself chills when she said it because she meant it.

"I love you too baby, but don't you ever get scared that what we have is too good to be true and one day we'll just vanish before each other's eyes and be nothing but a memory." Woo said.

Mecca didn't like what she'd heard. It was negative for no reason. It was unfair to the love they shared. Mecca shook her head no. "You mine until the end of time, and time don't ever end." Mecca said.

Then, they proceeded to lovemaking session part II. When the flashback poofed away like a cloud of dust, Mecca tried to reply to Woo' text message, but her phone disappeared from the palm of her hand.

Mecca roared with a hopeless rage. It was all a dream.

***

"What the hell were you thinking, chile?" Zeal asked, trembling. She was ready to smack lightning bolts from Zion, but Zillion restrained her.

"Mama calm down, that's not helping anything." Zillion said. Zeal through her hands up.

"She needs a good ass whooping, that's what she needs." Zeal said and shook her head disgracefully at Zion.

Zion bowed her tearful head and cried in shame. Zillion sighed. It affected her to see her child with her head hanging down.

"Ma could you excuse me and my child? We need some privacy." Zillion said.

Zeal grunted and sashayed her way onto the front porch where she sat lividly. Zillion plopped down next to Zion on the sofa. She wrapped her arm around Zion. Zion kept her head down. Zillion wrecked her brain for the right words to say. Shamir posted a video of Zion mastabating while they were having virtual sex via FaceTime. He claimed it was an accident, but he refused to delete it. Zillion had to report the video in order for it to be stripped down from the internet.

"I wish I would just die. I don't wanna live no more." Zion said.

Zillion gulped through the knot in her throat. "Baby don't talk like that." She said.

"Why not? It's true, my life is over anyway."

"I'm your mother and I'm saying otherwise. Your life has just begun. This little slip up needs to be a learning curve for you, not a pit stop."

"I wish I could press delete and all of this would just go away. I should've never trusted Shamir. That was so dumb of me."

"It's okay to have those feelings of hopelessness but you're going to have to learn to give people and their opinion your ass to kiss."

"That's easier said than done, mama. I'm a teenager my life revolves around people's opinions of me"

"Maybe so, but it's up to you to decide whose opinion is more important."

"Do you know one thing I get tired of hearing?"

"What's that Zion?"

"That I'm pretty for a dark skinned chick or I have pretty hair for a black girl, or that I don't act black at all. It's like just when I thought I found a boy that accepted me for me, he goes and betrays me in the worst way, to the point that I'll never trust again."

Zillion was speechless. Moments like those made her miss her father. He would know just what to say and do to make the whole situation better. He would know how to comfort Zion. Zillion wished she wasn't so helpless. She faulted herself for having a child too early, and having to raise a fatherless child. She tried to love her daughter as best she could. At times she overextended herself in order to make up for the absence of Zion's father, but even still somehow she always fell short. She and Zion set in silence for hours, just wallowing in their own despair. Zeal made them comfort food. Sloppy joe sandwiches with cheese and a jug of fruity red kool aid. They ate as a family in the living room without their usual banter. Their night was somber, sober, and unsettled. They all fell asleep binge watching How to Get Away With Murder.

The red wine didn't ease Zillion's heavy mind the way she had expected. Instead she sat on the balcony of her home she shared with her sixteen year old daughter and her sixty year old mother. Sade's a soldier of love resounded in the soft breeze. Moments as such always reminded her just how lonely she really was. The only man she'd ever trusted to give her body to was no man at all. He was a boy passing as a man, but regardless it didn't matter because he would be in prison for the rest of his life. Through her drunken mind, Zillion tried to remember those times she was blindly in love with her child's father, Rashawn, without feeling guilty or resentful for having those feelings. She came up short every time. He was her biggest mistake, though they'd moved passed it years ago, Zillion still felt a sickening feeling each time. There was no doubt in her mind about her love for her child. She didn't consider Zion a mistake, but she regretted the circumstances her daughter was born into. Zillion had been sheltered by her parents. Their strict determination to keep her in a child's place pushed her to rebel and sneak around with kids they tried to shield her from. Even in her adult years she had no experience of intimacy and love with a man. She had no desire to be with one. Zillion had learned to compartmentalize her emotions of loneliness, anger, and sadness. She'd overcome her desires of love, sex, and intimacy by consuming her time with academia and overachievement. Just when she thought she'd conquered the urges of her lonely heart, her despair came crashing into her like a hurricane. Undoubtedly, Zillion was an incredible therapist, she was one of the most distinguished in her profession. The therapy sessions she conducted were her ways of projecting happiness and true peace unto others, although that was something she'd never felt. If not her child's life, if not her devoted mother, if not her awards and great accomplishments, then what would be the answer to fulfill the brokenness she struggled to overcome? She wondered, but cringed at the thought that she might need therapy herself. As she sat in her outdoor lounge chair staring at the crescent moon, tears welled and fell from her almond eyes. She'd come to accept that the time had come for her to seek therapy for her own traumas, and maybe it would be great for her and Zion to do their sessions together. That way, Zion would see that her mother was no different from her after all.

***

One month later, Mecca sat in her studio awaiting her first client in nearly two months. She'd sketched out the tattoo idea they'd sent her. It was an eagle locked in the caress of a butterfly with a Japanese symbol that means unconditional love beneath it. Mecca knew by looking at the sketch that the client was heavily into spirit animals and symbolism. Still nothing could have prepared her for what she'd encountered in her studio that evening. It was true if you loved something let it go and if it's real then it would come back to you. Mecca looked as if she'd seen a ghost. Woo smiled uneasily under her gaze.

"Say something, why don't you?" Woo said.

Mecca's surprise had swiftly turned to anger. Her response to Woo was cold.

"Where the fuck have you been?"

Woo nodded her head, bounded by defeat.

"I was in Georgia. Savannah actually. My sister gave birth to my niece and I wanted to be there for her."

" Is that your final answer?"

"Mecca, I'm sorry for the way I left. It was spiteful and uncaused for. "

Mecca caught a knot in her throat. She wanted to spazz on Woo, but the remorse in Woo' eyes tamed her.

"I called you. I texted you. I even emailed you, damn near lost my goddamn mind and all you gotta say is sorry. That's real typical of you mane."

"Typical? Really Mecca? So you just so innocent and unsuspecting huh? "

"I never said I was innocent, but ain't I worthy gaddamn it? I couldn't get a simple reply, no don't worry Mecca I'm okay, or even a fuck you Mecca, I need some space, nothing?"

"You didn't want the life I wanted Mecca. I thought I was doing you a favor."

"Cut the bullshit, mane. Woo, why you here now?"

"I needed to make things right."

"By playing games with me and popping up at my shop out of the blue? Your level of reason is shitty as fuck Woo."

"The day we first met, you told me if I was ever in Memphis I should stop by your shop. You said no matter the tattoo you knew the perfect place to ink it on my body. Remember?"

"Damn right I do." Mecca said thinking of the anonymous note requesting that Mecca choose the perfect space on her body to ink the tattoo. It was making sense now, the whole little set up.

"Mecca, baby I'm sorry for the way I left things between us. It wasn't easy going that long without hearing your voice and seeing your face. I punished myself in order to no longer need you the way I did. I cried through a lot of sleepless nights wondering what hot thottie of the week had your attention. I suffered too, baby girl."

"If you had just picked up the phone..."

"Then what Mecca? You would have told me how much I wasn't worth the rest of your life? How much you wasn't ready to start a family? How I was suffocating you by asking you to place me as a first priority? That shit is for the birds Mecca. I don't wanna feel ashamed for asking for more out of my woman."

"Woo did you really want that shit? I mean do you really want that shit or were you just trying to tie me down, so you could have one up on other bitches?"

"Mecca I could really smack the taste from your mouth right now. Don't ever disrespect me like that."

Mecca could tell by the expression on Woo' face that she met every word. She decided to drop the subject.

"Are you trying to get a tattoo or nah?" Mecca asked.

"Where are you going to put it?"

"I don't think you ready for all that." Mecca said, intentionally challenging Woo, because Woo would never back down from a challenge.

"What?" Woo said, sucking her teeth. " Try me." Woo said, making herself and Mecca laugh out loud for the first time since their intense reunion.

Woo placed her bag on the counter and sat in the chair. Mecca gloved up and prepared her materials.

"Take those off." Mecca said tapping Woo' thigh. Woo looked at Mecca with a confused nervous expression.

"What do you mean?" Woo asked.

"I said what I said, but if you scared , don't even worry about it."

"Mecca stop playing games, where are you putting the tattoo?"

Mecca licked her lips and grinned. " On your vulva"

"On my pussy?! Mecca no. That shit gonna hurt too bad."

Mecca laughed. "I'm fucking with you. I'm going to put it on your lower abdominal leading towards the pussy."

Woo nodded. "I like that better."

"Loosen your trousers hoochie." Mecca said then winked at Woo. Woo slapped Mecca's thigh.

"You play way too much."

"Shut up, you deserve all my pettiness. I still ain't forgave you."

"Whatever, even though my heart was still broken I forgave you."

"Woo I don't think you forgave me. I think you took me back to punish me."

"I don't care what you think, Mecca. No matter what I did. I never fucking cheated on you."

"Yea well you may as well have. It would've been easier to move on. I could've bounced back from that shit."

"Oh really?"

"Yea, really."

"Mecca, I was m.i.a for three months. I'm certain that you found you some lil thotties to keep you occupied during my time away."

"That's all you think of me, huh? You---."

"Do my fucking tattoo!!" Woo screamed.

Mecca wanted to rock Woo' dome, but quieted herself. Thoughtfully, she reasoned that Woo had every reason to react the way that she had. Mecca had cheated on her in the prime of their relationship. She could only imagine the battles of insecurity and trust issues Woo faced. Mecca would have fled and never looked back if Woo had cheated on her. Woo was beautiful, outgoing, and strong. Mecca had to admit that Woo' fierce personality is what caused her to take Woo for granted. She saw Woo' vulnerability as she struggled to wiggle out of her jeans. The jeans seemed to be painted on. Mecca helped her slide out of them.

Mecca let Jhene Aiko sing about how much she was bitter and triggered, on the screen of her wall mounted television. Woo closed her eyes and counted in her head to distract herself from the pain of the needle. Mecca could smell Woo' temperature rising from the crests of her thighs. She wanted to drop her ink gun and go to town on Woo right then and there. Actually she strongly considered making a move, but she controlled her urge. Mecca added details that Woo hadn't asked for, but she knew Woo would appreciate the added detail. The floral frame, and the coloring looked extravagant on Woo's pretty brown skin.

"Oh my goodness. Mecca, it is beautiful." Woo sang as she admired her new body art in the full length mirror. She couldn't contain her happiness. She gave Mecca a tight genuine hug.

"One ah dem, love. Glad you like it, love." Mecca replied.

"How do I repay you for this?" Woo asked in all seriousness.

"Treat me to dinner. I'm starving."

Woo nodded flirtatiously. "I got you. Burger King on me." She said, laughing. Mecca smacked her on the ass. Woo rolled her eyes, and gave Mecca the stank face.

"You been wanting to do that all night." Woo said.

Mecca shrugged. "You damn skippy. That pussy is still mine."

"Yeahh, see no. There goes your true motive seeping out." Woo replied.

Mecca smirked. "Girl please, it's a fact."

"Mecca, I didn't come here for this. It took me a while to return to myself, but I'm back on my square and I'm not falling off. When I first met you. I thought that you were so fucking sexy. I put you on an instant pedestal because you were something new to my senses. But my attraction was built off lust. And honey, lemme tell you now that I got that shit out of my system, I see you for who you are, and it makes me feel silly for thinking that you could ever truly love me past what's between my legs."

Woo's outburst struck Mecca like a knife to the heart. She was seeing Woo in a different light. The woman she loved had returned to her as a stranger. Months of waiting and postponing her way of life had been a complete waste. Woo never even believed Mecca loved her. In fact she was ashamed of her attraction to Mecca. She was so ashamed that she couldn't even say that she loved Mecca. Which was a sure dagger to Mecca's heart. Mecca had lost her appetite. Woo had made her feel as though everything she'd experienced, every emotion, the sickness and pain, was all in vain. Mecca had lost time that she could not get back, and that was enough to cure any trace of lovesickness she had left. She'd gotten what she needed from Woo all along. Closure. Mecca decided against telling Woo about her new therapy journey. She didn't want to achieve any sympathy from Woo. She didn't need cool points in Woo's book. The time had come for them to close out that chapter.

Mecca did, however, apologize to Woo for the drama she'd put her through. She also made it clear that her love was true. Woo accepted Mecca's apology, and thanked her for inspiring her to go deeper within herself. Woo confessed to Mecca that she had taken a vow of celibacy and that she'd hoped to keep that vow for two years. Mecca was amazed, because she couldn't help but reminisce about the sweet love they'd shared. Her mouth watered at the remembrance of Woo's juicebox. They departed with an intimate hug. Both were satisfied with the closure they'd gained.

***

Four nights later, Mecca lied awake in her bed at 2am. The burden of lost love she'd once felt had been lifted. Her mind was clear for the first time in months. She'd replayed the reunion between her and Woo several times, and she concluded that she was not in love with Woo, but the potential of who Woo could become. She'd placed Woo on a pedestal, and in turn Woo had done the same to her. The disconnect was inevitable when neither could meet each other's expectations.

Mecca was confused by the number that appeared on her call screen.

"What up?" Mecca answered.

"Hey miss cocky." Kiana replied.

Mecca frowned at the phone.

"Mane look, who is this?"

"Oh wow you got so many freaks you can't keep up huh?"

Mecca ended the call. She wasn't in the mood for games. It frustrated her that grown women would rather play games than just get straight to the point and not waste each other's time.

"I'm sorry Mecca. It's Kiana. I wanna see you again." Kiana said in a message she'd sent to Mecca's phone.

Mecca smiled. Kiana hit her with a proposition she could use that night. A fuck buddy with no strings attached.

"Pull up." Mecca replied with a smiley emoji.

One hour later, Mecca played her turn-a-bitch-out playlist. The sweet scent of berry candles filled the air.

Mecca had the strawberries, the whipped cream, and the bowl of melted chocolate ready on the low sitting coffee table. Showtime. The doorbell rang. Kiana came inside smiling ear to ear.

"Aww, this is sweet, love." Kiana said.

Mecca closed the door behind her, and pushed Kiana's back against it. Wrapping her legs around Mecca's waist, Kiana dropped her overnight bag to the floor. Mecca licked and sucked Kiana's neck like a vampire. She wasn't in the mood for talking. In seconds Kiana's furry slippers were across the room, and her neon biker shorts were on the floor. Mecca slid her fingers inside Kiana and worked her love tunnel. Kiana was the pot of sauce and Mecca's fingers were the stirring spoon. Kiana moaned into Mecca's mouth. She was wide open, thrusting her hips and slow winding against Mecca's motion. Kiana didn't come to play. She wanted to show Mecca she could get down too. She pushed Mecca off of her, and backed her onto the couch. It was simply time for her to return the favor. Hesitant, Mecca clenched up.

Kiana looked up at her and smiled. "I'm grown. I got you." She said.

Mecca received Kiana's tongue action with deep satisfaction. She did alright for a newbie. It was on and poppin' from there. They didn't stop until the sun rose, and they were both sticky with sex juices and chocolate. By the time they were done they were laid up in Mecca's bedroom. Although they fell asleep in each other's arms, Mecca was straight up with Kiana about her intentions. She let Kiana know that they were strictly fuck buddies, and that Kiana could be her sneaky link as long as they respected each other's boundaries. Kiana laughed at Mecca's straight forwardness, but she agreed.

***

Two months later, Mecca sat on Zillion's therapy couch. Zillion raved about Mecca's progress. They'd come so far in a short time span. Their session had more of a homie vibe. Zillion found herself laughing heartily at Mecca' perspectives on life. They'd each looked forward to the next time they'd meet again. Mecca had even brought wings to their session, and they spent two hours talking and eating. They both agreed that whenever the conversation exceeded one hour whatever else was said was off the record. Mecca enjoyed Zillion's energy. She had an innocence about her, yet she was more mature than any woman she knew. Tonya was the main cheerleader for their relationship, but Mecca wouldn't cross that line. She liked having Zillion as a therapist and a homie. It was also refreshing to have a platonic bond with a woman whom she found to be attractive. Their attraction and the respect was mutual, and that was something each of them wanted to protect. Who knew? Down the line, that'd probably make for an unbreakable course of love and matrimony.

Black Amarucan Queens

By

Damita Taylor

"Yea, Yea. Give me all my mothafuckin loot, whores!" Genesis yelled boastfully as she swept several hundred dollars from the money stash on the dressing room floor. She was busting heads in the intense dice game. She and six other ladies played before the show.

"I should be all you bitches pimps. I swear, cuz y'all folks just throwing me y'all money." Genesis talked cash money smack when one of the young ladies crapped out again and had to put her money up.

"Chill out, G. You wildin." Tatiyana shook her head. She wasn't a gambler, and it wrecked her nerves the way Genesis and the other girls put up thousands just for the fun of it. Genesis on the other hand got a rush from betting large sums of money for the price of a great reward or an even greater risk. Genesis was daring like that. Money wasn't her master, she mastered it.

Saweetie *My Type* was like a soundtrack for the organized chaos inside the dressing room. Blunt smoke clouded the room. An air of liquor concocted with various perfumes and natural body heat swarmed the room's air. Half naked women in exotic wear partook in whatever routine that was needed in order for them to get right for the night's show.

"Bitch done came up and we ain't even hit the floor yet." Sensei, the eldest of the ladies said as she high-fived Genesis with genuine admiration.

Genesis gloated, "I'm big mama, these worsem ass hoes my kids." Everyone in earshot laughed. Even Genesis' biggest hater and the worst sore loser ever, Drip, had to give it up.

" Ayo bebes it's showtime, is you ready?!" Stackz, the club manager emerged, and gave the ladies the cue that playtime was over. She was a caramel complexioned New Orleans native, who had big boobies, big braids, big money. And a big mean glock to protect her business and her workers by any means necessary. Stackz made it so that no violence or any shiesty occurrences for that matter occurred anywhere near or around her club.

"Aite bet !" Genesis said happily as she counted two grand from the dice game alone. She winked at Tatiyana. A clear signal that it was going to be an upstanding night for them financially. Tatiyana saluted her, popped a perc and straightened Ariel, a nickname she'd given her red wavy wig.

Filthy Rich Niggas better known as FRNz we're celebrating one of their FRNz' birthday. They had the club booming. An appointed security guard was in every corner. In less than two hours most of the girls had raked in at least a grand.

Tatiyana and Genesis were quick on their feet. They created a clever scheme to filter out the imposters and scavenger up the real huncho. It didn't take long. Since both Tati and Genesis held ninja like qualities when it came to weaving through the fakers and flashy show offs of their environment.
Megan The Stallion Sex Talk shook the club. Booties were shaking, titties jiggled beneath money showers. King stood out. He was a subtle playa. His cuban link chain-fourteen karats, and the presidential rollie on his wrist symbolized his self awareness and confidence in his own skin. His good looks were the cherry on top. Tatiyana made the first move. She played it smooth and approached King with a bottle of Ace of Spades. He gazed down at her with sex in his eyes. Tatiyana smiled, she peeped him eating her alive with his eyes.

"You like what you see?" Tatiyana asked, teasingly.

He squinted his eyes as he softly grabbed her wrist. "Is that for me?" King asked.

"It can be." She said.

"What is it gon' take for me to make it mine?" He asked.

Tatiyana spun around in search of Genesis. She smiled when she saw Genesis making her way toward the VSOP Room. Genesis glanced over her shoulder and spoke a language with her eyes that only they would understand. Their plan was locked and loaded.

"Follow me." Tatiyana said, handing King the bottle of Ace of Spades. She grabbed his hand and guided him through the tight knit crowd.

King was pleasantly surprised to see Genesis sitting on the classic pink leather lounge sofa. The interior of the room was pink and gold. The decorations were an ode to an early sixties New Orleans style club.

"Shit yea, the big fella looking out for a nigga. I see." He said, rubbing his hands together.

Tatiyana glanced at Genesis and circled around King like she was presenting a grand prize on a game show.

"Look what I found, friend." Tatiyana said.

King cocked his head back, amused by the antic.

"I don't know why you did that, now I want him all to myself." Genesis said.

"I feel that, but I figured we'd share, friend." Tatiyana said.

"Big facts, ain't no fun unless the homie get some." King said.

They purposely ignored him.

"I don't wanna share. I bet a stack that I can make him bust before you do." Genesis said.

"Aite double up. Make that two stacks." Tatiyana said.

King' brows furrowed, it was obvious that he wasn't used to being treated like a sexual object.

Genesis and Tatiyana had him right where they wanted him. Eating out of their palms.

"Hm. Let's ask him. Who do you think got the freakiest tricks?" Genesis asked.

King shrugged. "I don't know but I put up twenty-five hundred my damn self."

Genesis and Tatiyana hid their excitement. They'd accomplished their main goal. It didn't matter who made him cum. By the time they rolled out a few tricks he'd forget about their silly competition, but the money would be theirs regardless.

"Rock paper scissors for first dibs." Tatiyana said.

Genesis almost burst out laughing. Tatiyana played too much, but she went along. King dropped down on the sofa, sitting with the posture of a king as he popped open the Ace and sipped straight from the bottle. He tossed two bands on the table like it was nothing. Tatiyana and Genesis pretended to be oblivious as they rocked paper, scissored it out.

"Rock paper scissor shoot!"

Genesis was up first. Her rock beat out Tati' scissors. She purposely took her time kissing his neck. She helped him out of his shirt, and straddled his lap.

Tati was over it, "What the fuck, G? Nah see, you gotta get straight to it." She said, making Genesis get out of the way. Tatiyana went to town on King's piece. She sucked and deep throated it like it was a pie eating race. King moaned and cussed his satisfaction. Genesis barely helped. She tickled his sack and fingered his booty. He bust in under five minutes. Tatiyana and King exchanged contacts. They would most definitely meet again.

Back at their two bedroom apartment, Genesis and Tatiyana counted their earnings for the night. They raked in six thousand altogether. It was undoubtedly a good night for them financially. Still, they locked away their cash in their personal safe. They both sat there on the floor of Genesis' bedroom with calculated expressions. The money they were making at the club started to feel like chump change. They wanted more. They wanted out of the Pyramid Strip Junt. They worked the club since they were eighteen and nineteen, now at Twenty-three and Twenty-four they aspired for a new lifestyle. As much as they loved her, they

109

didn't wanna be thirty-two still dancing like Entice. It was time for them to boss up.

"I hate how dicks look." Genesis said.

Tatiyana rolled her eyes, and blazed up. She puffed a few times before passing it to Genesis.

"What's your number?" Tati asked.

"Fool, look in your damn phone."

"Not your phone number. I'm not talking about that."

"Okay, so what you mean what's my number? What are you asking me?"

"What amount of money would it take to get you to leave the Pyramid?"

Genesis understood Tati' question completely. She reflected for a moment before she answered. The blunt slowed her mind, and allowed her to zone in on what was important. Long term, somewhere in the future she wanted to travel the entire continent of Africa, but the main attraction for her was Egypt. She was obsessed with the history of Egypt and how it developed the way of the world through science, art, food, religion, status symbols, and life principles. She knew it only took twenty thousand for the dream to come true. But that was a consumer based goal. Tatiyana was asking for her estimate from an owner standpoint.

"One hundred thousand." Genesis replied.

The young women locked eyes. Their thirst to get rich was uncanny. Being around niggas like FRNz and other go getters sparked a flame within them. It was time to up the ante. They weren't foolish enough to rob the bank, they'd seen what the end result of that type of action was, thanks to the film Set it Off. However, in a game where nobody gave you anything, the next best move was to take what you wanted. It was time to get down and dirty in a real street way. Genesis and Tatiyanna were up until eight o'clock am mapping out a plan to take down the Filthy Rich Niggas.

***

The first step was to get their hands on some pistols. They weren't the foolish kind. They were extremely smart and street savvy. They knew who the hook up was for the pistols, but they also knew not to drop into the territory and not know how to use one. That being said, they took a couple trips to the gun range. They learned how to properly hold the gun, reload, unload, and pull the trigger. They were naturals, they hit their targets effortlessly. In the midst of all of this, they continued to revise their strategy. Target practice became a hobby for them.

One month later, they made a visit to their connect, Mookie. Mookie was a female gun seller. The most respected in the underground market, because she was legit in the way she sold her weapons. She didn't sell to anybody. Every prospective buyer had to pass her tests or else she rejected them.

Mookie' Gun house was ducked off in an isolated house atop a hill. Surveillance cameras were everywhere. Genesis and Tatiyana arrived, lowkey in their ball caps and dark shades. They'd borrowed Tatiyana' granddad' old car. Mookie watched them on the monitors and buzzed them in before Tati's fist could even touch the door.

The house was basically a makeshift shooting range and gun shop all in one. Glocks, uzis, techs, and revolvers were pinned against mantels behind a bullet proof glass wall. Mookie sat in the living room area eating a bowl of pork and beans with white bread. She was an odd woman. She had a wide gap. A blonde bald fade. One gray eye and one dark brown eye. She was tall, but slim. She wore a neon fleece bulletproof vest for fashion.

"Come in ladies, have a seat." Mookie said, her voice was heavy and firm. She washed down her lunch with a colt .45. Mookie was just different. She'd been tried many times and everytime she was proved to be undefeated. Rumors circulated that she knew voodoo, and that's what kept her protected.

"What up Mook!" They greeted her, then shook her hand, respectfully, and removed their shades.

"I'm solid, I'm fluid." Mookie replied.

Tati and Genesis gave her a blank stare as they sat on her thrift store couch. Mookie was unmoved by their silence. She went about watching Peaky Blinders, disregarding their presence. They shrugged and watched along with her. Unbeknownst to them, they'd just entered the first phase of Mookie' test. Patience. Patience was important, because true warriors didn't rush to kill. A true soldier wasn't pressed to harm another. Tatiyana and Genesis didn't mind the wait, nohow, they weren't in a rush. Plus, it was common courtesy to adapt to the energy of the territory you entered. Also, Peaky Blinders was gangster. After two hours, Mookie paused the show.

"Damn it was just getting good." Genesis said, and Tati nudged her in the side.

Mookie watched them eerily. Her eyes were cold and intimidating. It sent chills through Tati, the way Mook didn't even blink. She was like a statue.

"You know why I don't like hair?" Mookie asked them. They were quiet, hesitant to respond.
"I asked a question, but don't all speak at once."

"Nah Mook, how would we know that." Genesis replied. She and Tati locked eyes sensing that was probably a terrible response.

"That's fair." Mookie said. "You don't know me, so how would you know that. You don't know me, but somehow you trust me. Why is that?" Mookie asked, tossing them a curveball.

Tatiyana and Genesis stayed silent. They simply didn't know what to say.

"Hmph. When I was six years old my daddy did my hair as I sat between his legs on the front porch. I

114

had long hair down to my back, and believe it or not daddy was an excellent braider. Daddy was also a street nigga. He was a known banger and a money guy. But you know in that game. In this game here, it be enemies. Daddy had enemies, like I got a lot of enemies. Except daddy' enemies succeeded. They drove by our house in a raggedy ass tahoe and blew my daddy brains out right behind me. Two shots. One to the pineal gland and one to the artery. Needless to say, I ain't never wanna get my hair done ever since. Cause it reminds me of the day my king was caught slippin'. I don't ever wanna get caught slippin behind no goddamn hair. Can y'all feel me?"

The tension in the room needed a chainsaw to cut through it. It was so thick and breathtaking that all Tati and Genesis could do was nod their heads, dumbfoundedly.

"Y'all some beautiful motherfuckas, if I may say so myself." Mookie said.

"Thank you, Mook." Genesis replied. Tati blew her breath and rolled her eyes. She wanted to tell Genesis to stop responding where it wasn't needed.

"Nooo, don't thank me. That's God's work. Thank God. God creates beautiful things. All the ugly shit is man made. Like these guns. I hate guns." Mookie said.

Genesis was about to speak, but Tati touched her knee, stopping her.

"Follow me ladies." Mookie said. Phase two was in motion. Most people failed phase two. Ironically enough they believed it was immoral and cruel. Tati and Genesis followed her down the short narrow hallway to her backyard that was setup for target practice. The first target was a white male wearing a ski mask. Mookie gave each of them a go at him.

"Impressive." She said as she examined their results.

She pinned up the second target. It was an older black lady carrying a grocery bag. Tatiyana and Genesis looked to each other and shook their heads in unison.

"What is y'all scared?" Mookie asked, daringly.

"Nah, it's just that's not a necessary target." Tatiyana spoke up.

116

Mookie shrugged. "Okay, that's fair." She said. Then she pinned up a pitbull. Tatiyana and Genesis had a go at it.

"I'm impressed." Mookie said.

Lastly, she put up a white woman wearing a Maga hat. Genesis laughed and shot it just for fun, but Tatiyana refused. That concluded phase two. They'd earned Mookie's respect without even knowing it. Many people didn't think twice about the targets they shot until the dog was pinned up, or a lion, or a cat. Mookie found it quite sickening to know that an animal got more consideration for a chance at life than an actual human being. It's not that she had anything against animals. She was an animal lover, it's just that she expected humans to see themselves in other humans, and think twice about their reaction.

Phase III, they were back on the thrift store couches inside Mookie's living room area. Mookie blindfolded each of them with bandannas. She instructed them to pull the gun apart then piece it back together.

"If you can't do the shit with your eyes closed you don't need one." Mookie said.

Nevertheless they passed. They left Mookie' house with new pistols and a newfound alliance.

***

"Shit is getting real, G." Tatiyana said as she blew blunt smoke into the air of an empty bedroom. They were inside their hideout . A small-rundown house they'd bought from a hopeless seller. The night had finally come. The plan was in full throttle. Their hearts were racing. It was stone quiet at their location. The sound of crickets chirping gave them a natural ambience. The wind passing through could be heard through their thin windows. Cars drove by here and there. Their senses were wide open. In a few hours they would be meeting up with King. The reality of the situation had finally dawned on them. A single mistake could cause them everything. It was a gamble, but it was a gamble they were willing to take. The risk was high, but the reward was even higher.

Genesis paced the room with venom in her eyes. Tatiyana had only seen Genesis that serious once. She and Genesis were no strangers to the streets. They'd been in group homes, juvenile detention, and a facility together. They weren't physically twins, but their souls were identical. Blood couldn't make them any closer.

"Out of sight out of mind. Don't let this shit psyche you out, Tati." Genesis said with a chilled sense of calmness. Adrenaline was her fuel, the nervousness that tickled her shoulders couldn't shake her.

Tatiyana was terrified. She wasn't like Genesis. Whereas, Genesis could see the consequences and still push the envelope, Tatiyana was more cautious. She wasn't going to fold. She was more worried about the outcome. Who would come out on top? That's what she questioned. Even if they did prevail and got away without a scratch, it wouldn't be victorious if the cops were to get involved. When it was all said and done Tatiyana didn't want them to have to look over their shoulders in paranoia at every single turn. Genesis blazed a second blunt and hogged it for a minute before she passed it on. She recognized the fearful energy Tati was giving off, and decided to trade a war story they shared.

" You remember that night in South memphis…" As soon as those words left Genesis' mouth, Tatiyana' lips quivered, her eyes watered.

Genesis continued, "We were just children. Remember that?"

Tatiyana nodded her head. The tears fell like raindrops.

"Dem niggas tried to kill us. Rico choked Jade to death with that goddamn crowbar. They had the gasoline ready for us. We was next. We was running for our lives in the heat of the night like some goddamn runaway slaves, Tati."

"I remember, G." Tati cried.

"How long did it take for them to find Jade body in that fucking field?" Genesis asked, her face drenched with tears.

Tati shook her head defeatedly. The sorrow remained. Justice never served for her cousin Jade. "How long, Tati?" Genesis asked, pleadingly.

"Ten days."

"So what does that tell you about this world when it come to us?"

Tati shrugged. " They don't give a fuck about us."

" We here for a reason, Tati. These niggas don't give a fuck about us. Don't nobody give a fuck about you until you build a place for yourself in this world. Nah, fuck that. I ain't got no fear. I don't feel no remorse. Nobody gave me shit, so I'm gon' take what I need." Genesis said, enraged. "So, answer me this. Would you rather be the victim or the fucking suspect?"

Tatiyana exhaled, and nodded with a newfound encouragement. Genesis had given Tatiyana the motivation she needed. She reminded her of her reason.

" This is for Jade. This is for us." Tati said, wiping her tears from her face.

" Say less." Genesis added.

10:30 pm, Downtown Memphis. Genesis and Tatiyana rolled up to King' luxury condo. They wore short trench coats over their sexy and revealing skirt sets. They wore dark shades to conceal their faces. King had his place set up real nice for them. He had seafood, music playing, and a liquor game in mind. He walked around shirtless in his fitted gray joggers. He smelled like he'd just gotten out the shower. Tatiyana and Genesis wore their poker faces. He never would have expected their true motives for being there. They weren't there to waste time with food and play. He was no friend of theirs. They hung their trench coats on the coat rack, and took their seats in the fancy lounge chairs made for a bachelor. Genesis ate a few shrimp from the seafood boil. Tati had no appetite at all. King dropped down next to her and put his arm around her waist.

"Why so shy, sexy girl? I did all this for you and you ain't touched a thing." He noted.

Tati smiled bashfully and winked at him.

" I'm not a seafood kinda girl. You should have asked me what I liked."

"Aite bet. I deserve that L. Will you forgive me?"

Tati smiled, seductively. " You're good love. She said rubbing his inner thigh.

"Aite fasho." He said, then looked over at Genesis. He smirked and shook his head. She was in her own world it seemed. She nodded her head and tapped to the beat of the music.

Tatiyana picked the card game up from the table.

"You wanna get us full and drunk huh?"

King chuckled. " It's called being a great host."

Tatiyana gave Genesis a look.

"Where's your bathroom?" Genesis asked.

"Down the hall to your right." He replied.

Once she was out of ear and eyeshot, Genesis began to roam the condo. She slipped off into his master bedroom, in search of his money stash. She came up short. She then went into his study and rambled some more. After about six minutes of lurking she hit a jackpot. His safe was hidden behind his bookshelf. Genesis grunted her excitement. She went into the bathroom just to save face. She flushed the toilet, washed her hands and sprayed just in case King brought up any suspicion about her taking so long to return.

King and Tati we're sharing laughter with stars in their eyes when Genesis returned.

"Oh okay, am I interrupting the party, newlyweds?" Genesis said, breaking up their cutesy moment.

Tati gave Genesis the look. Genesis laughed and sat next to King. They made a sandwich with him in between.

"I got enough for both y'all. Believe that." King said.

Genesis eyed him seductively, " I bet you do, daddy." She said. The words tasted like shit rolling from her mouth. She cringed.

King laid back like a king. The liquor was hitting him. He was relaxed and ready to get nasty with the two beautiful ladies on his arm.

Tatiyana massaged him, until he couldn't take anymore.

"Damn girl, you some else with those hands." He said.

Tatiyana put her finger to his lips. She pulled Genesis closer, and they began tongue kissing him together. The sensation caused him to moan.

"Damn, that's wassup." He breathed.

Genesis attempted to stand up, but Tati stopped her. Genesis gave her the look. Tati stripped bare naked. Genesis followed suit. King looked mesmerized by their fierce sexy curves and succulent breasts.

"Beautiful bitches." He said.

Tati slapped him. He took it on the chin. Tatiyana knew that they were cut for time. She was done stalling. King was right where they wanted him. With his dick in his hand. They could have ended him at that very moment, but Tati wanted to sedate him even more. She wanted him so tranquil that he'd be very much defenseless. She began to ride him and sex him until he exploded.
When he opened his eyes from his orgasm. Two pistols were aimed at him. Tatiyana had moved from his reach. Genesis passed Tatiyana the other gun. They were both ready to shoot.

"What the fuck? Are you bitches nuts?" He asked, appalled. His chest heaved sporadically. Terror mixed with rage was in his eyes.

Their gun had silencers. Mookie suggested they get them. There were no sounds when they shattered his body with eight bullets. Arm, leg, head, arm leg. They used his face to unlock his phone completely. The code to the safe was the founding day of the Filthy Rich Niggas. They bagged the cash, got dressed and vamped.

***

"Crime pays." Genesis said.

She and Tati had spent three days at their hideout counting money. They'd passed their goal. They probably miscounted a few stacks but came up with half a mill. Their eyes were red and wide from sleep deprivation. They were overwhelmed with their new riches. All they could do was stare at the massive rows of money.

"We official now, we conquered our first mission." Tati said

"What you mean first mission? We can wash our hands with this shit. We got the money and the nigga ghost. Literally." Genesis said.

"We made a big mess, G. Don't get comfortable. A body in this game ain't shit but a trail. Niggas gon' be after us."

"How? In what way? Don't nobody know we was there. Our faces were concealed with the wigs and those dark ass shades. You overthinking it." Genesis said.

"No G, you underestimating the circumstance we under. Niggas gon put bounties out for their big homie. You don't think niggas talk? I can guarantee you he told somebody he bagged us." Tati said.

" But we got his phone, remember?"

"Yea Aite."

"Aite what? Don't hold back , speak your mind."

"Nah cause your knuckle head self don't never listen. You think you know everything."

"Aw I think I know everything, but you the one mad cause I'm not rocking with your point of view."

"I said Aite G, so drop it."

" Say less."

Tati huffed and laid back on her hands, glaring at the ceiling. Genesis lurked through King' phone while Tati fumed over their disagreement. Genesis began shaking uncontrollably. The information she found via King' iMessages spooked her senseless.

"Tati, oh my god, Tati."

"Girl what? Why are you trippin now?"

" You have to see this!"

"Quit playing, G I'm not for the funny shit right now."

Genesis held up the phone. "Tati, look!" Genesis screamed with a frightened expression.

The latest messages were full of pictures of teenage girls, who were either runaways or listed missing persons. The messages discussed prices and possible locations to sell the girls for trafficking. The addresses were detailed in a cryptic way. One would have to be hipped to the hood lingo in order to make out what they were saying.

"This is our scapegoat, this is our out. This shit is foul, but it would turn the attention from us." Tatiyana said.

Genesis was speechless. She shook her head in disbelief.

They made an anonymous call to the police department. They gave out addresses, nicknames, and other key details. They destroyed the phone and trashed it afterwards.

***

Midnight, they were at a Waffle House in East Memphis when the news broke that the Filthy Rich Niggas were raided and taken into custody on felonious charges. Fifty-eight young girls were rescued from the secret brothels and trap houses the FRNz had set up throughout the city.

They couldn't believe their eyes as they watched the madness on the tiny flat screen, the Waffle House workers had set up on top the counter. They felt a sense of pride, but they were also relieved. The heat was off of them. They knew their best move was to go on as if nothing had changed. Back to the Pyramid.

***

It was another lit night at the Pyramid Strip Junt. Stackz had given the ladies a surprise bonus. They had themselves a celebration inside their dressing room. Genesis and Tati were ecstatic because once again the threat of suspicion was directed away from them. Stories of many of the FRNz skipping town or folding under the pressure of the system kept unfolding. There were even bounties on their heads because of their dealings with the selling young girls. The young women had not expected the rabbit hole to be that deep when they made their scheme. However, the information they'd found in King' phone exposed a glossary of secrets and hidden agendas. Tati and Genesis got rid of the phone before they were caught up in a whirlwind of havoc and scandal.

The crowd was a mixture of women and men. It was Pride weekend, and the rainbow family was turnt. The cashflow was more than generous. The vibe was upbeat and unique. Some of the men gave the strippers a run for their money with their pole dancing skills. Tory Lanez record screamed to the parking lot that he hadn't been broke in a minute.

"Your people know how to party, girl. I feel like I'm in Vegas somewhere. " Tatiyana said.

Genesis laughed. "And do." She added.

Genesis had never shied away from her sexual and emotional attraction to women, although her lifestyle as a dancer made it challenging for her to remain true to herself. It was always a joy to her when her community came out to show love and simply have fun at the Pyramid, which was not often.

A group of trans women stole the show with their Kash Doll For Everybody and Ice Me Out medley. The crowd went wild. The dancers were living their best life vibing with the gays and having a little girl on girl action with the women. Tati ended up dancing in the section with a group of gay men who had bought her drinks. Genesis was in her own world, clapping her cheeks and feeling sexy. She could feel eyes burning through her. It made her feel sexier not knowing where to spot her secret admirer. She discreetly looked over her shoulder trying to spot her little spy, when a familiar scent greeted her nostrils. The touch sent electricity through her body. The voice made her creamy inside.

"I missed you, my love." Sasha said, her lips were pressed against Genesis' neck.

Genesis didn't turn around. She waited. She cupped Sasha' face and winded her hips against her, enjoying the sensation of Sasha rubbing and groping her backside.

"I missed you more." Genesis said.

Sasha twirled Genesis around to face her. "I know I should've called, but I wanted to surprise you." She said. Sasha was Malian, a native of Mali. She'd left America to return home to tend to her sick mother until she regained her health. Sasha had done her best to keep in touch with Genesis while she was away but the time difference made it near impossible. Sasha' accent and her demeanor always made Genesis swoon and melt on the inside. She brought out Genesis' sweet and mushy side which was rare that anyone saw.

" It don't even matter. I'm just happy to have you here in my arms, baby." Genesis said, as she hugged Sasha' waist.

Sasha stood back. Genesis silky light blue ponytail made her look like an anime character to Sasha. Sasha made a funny face, causing Genesis to feel slightly insecure. Sasha was no stranger to Genesis lifestyle, although she often encouraged Genesis to land a different hustle, she never knocked her for being a stripper. Their love was unconditional, and Sasha understood that there were barriers Genesis was up against which forced her to sell herself short. Genesis was beautiful, witty, and talented in more ways than one, but she was building a life from scratch. She never had proper parental guidance. The child care system failed her. The streets had almost killed her. The pyramid was a safe haven. It was her and Tati' first home. Stackz protected the girls like a genuine mother figure. She ran her club with an iron fist, and led by example how to be a strong independent woman. It was up to the young ladies rather they took heed and followed in her footsteps or not. No matter that many people looked down on the strip club industry. Stackz ran a business, and there was no business without supply in demand. Strippers and fun girls existed because there was a demand for them. People, men and women paid good money to get that sensual and erotic experience the Pyramid Strip Junt provided. Sasha was a business woman herself. She ran Top Shelf Braids and Locs, a successful braiding shop. She was no stranger to the struggle, she built her business from the ground up. She'd slept on park benches and bummed leftovers from fast food spots too when money was low and she had nowhere to go. It would make her hypocrite to stand there to judge or criticize Genesis for her position. No, she wasn't judging at all, she just knew Genesis. Sasha saw through the fake lashes, colorful weaves, and lusty attire. Sasha saw through Genesis' tough act. She could still see the innocence in Genesis. She could read her eyes like they were one of her favorite books she'd read a thousand times over. Along with that, it was an instinct she inhabited during her days of homelessness to study the body languages and voiceless expressions of those surrounding her. She knew when something was off, especially when it came to her woman.

"What's wrong, baby?" Genesis asked.

"Is it something you wanna tell me or are we holding secrets now?" Sasha asked.

Genesis frowned. " No it's not like that, Sasha calm down you just got here, let's just enjoy our moment." She said.

Sasha clenched her jaws. She couldn't help it. It was second nature, a defense mechanism for her to feel out her environment before she let her guards down. Something was off with Genesis, and though it came off as an overreaction, her ability to shut down and retreat from those funny feeling vibes is what kept her alive on the streets. It was a mentality she and Genesis shared. Genesis just played hers more charismatically. Genesis had every intention of telling Sasha everything. About the murder and all. She trusted Sasha with her life. Sasha had proved her loyalty a thousand times over, so it was only right.

Sasha looked from Genesis to the happenings around her.

"Isis, I don't take chances to be made a fool. Not for love not for anything. But you know this." Sasha said.

"I know Sasha, but you gotta trust me, baby. I'll tell you everything, but right now is not the time or place." Genesis said.

Sasha recognized that glitch of terror in Genesis' eyes, and decided to drop it. " Okay if you say later is best, we'll discuss later, my love." Sasha said.

Sensei waved them over to the booth she occupied with a few of her homegirls from around the way. Tati was center stage with four other strippers by then, throwing ass for a crowd of thirsty looking studs and fems.

" Look at the lovebirds, how cute is y'all. If y'all ever need a unicorn keep me in mind." Sensei said. Semi joking, semi flirtatious.

Genesis wrapped Sasha' arms around her waist protectively. "All mine. I'm stingy with this one." Genesis replied.

Sensei gave an approving nod. "As you should be, baby girl." She stated. Then handed them both shots of Patron. They made a toast to the good life, and drank in unisom. Genesis and Sensei poked fun at some of their co-workers and laughed about good old times. Sasha sat back with Genesis in her lap, simply happy to have her girl.

***

Detective Aaliyah Hopes stared unflinchingly at the bulletin board of one hundred and forty-two missing black girls. Their faces were engraved in her mind by that point. Their names echoed inside her head like a sad old song. What started out as a fiery mission towards justice, had become an impossible dream deferred. However, Aaliyah was still relentless in her pursuit to bring those children home and give their families closure. It'd been a cold and lonely road, but a flame had been ignited. Thanks to the anonymous tip her department received from an unknown young woman. Fifty of what used to be two hundred young faces were removed from the bulletin. The race to victory had just begun. A liver full of Jack Daniels distorted her judgment, yet her optimism was intensified. She couldn't have been sure, but she was willing to take the risk in order to achieve her die hard goal. She wanted to confront the anonymous girl. She'd gone the extra mile to locate the hideout without anyone knowing. She'd followed the young women for days against their knowledge.

***

Sasha ate her Waffle House All Star dinner with a careful precision while listening to Genesis and Tati recount the events that led up to and what resulted after their money heist. They talked about the scheme as if it was a century old. Sasha tuned in judgment free. She was no stranger to homicide. She was grateful that they came out on top. Though it gave them bragging rights, that outcome wasn't to be taken for granted, because some of the most thorough and seasoned hustlers had less fortunate fates in the life of crime.

"But I think Tati slick wanted the nigga for real." Genesis said, as an afterthought. The fact that Tati went out her way to have actual intercourse with King when he was already in the losing corner didn't sit well with Genesis. She believed Tati had real life feelings for King.

" I didn't want him. I mean he was fine, but I wasn't attached." Tati said, matter of factly.

"So why did you give the nigga the pussy when we could have just murked him right then and there. He was already lacking. " Genesis said.

Tati ate the chocolate chips out of her waffles. She didn't appreciate the way Genesis put her on the spot in front of Sasha. "Bitch you love to show out. Why you gotta bring this up now? You had all that time to say some and you just now bring it up in front Sasha." Tati replied.

" Whatever bitch, just hope your ass ain't pregnant with a dead man's baby, cause the nigga sholl didn't pull out." Genesis said.

Tati shivered. Genesis knew how to push her buttons, and she hated that. It was antics like that, that made her question Genesis' true motive toward her sometimes. It was remarks like that which made her rethink their bond. "Bitch if you wanna take this shit outside just say that." Tati said. She was seeing red.

"Say less, come on then." Genesis said. She lived for drama, and welcomed every challenge. It wasn't her fault Tati couldn't take a joke. They rose from the kitchen table ready to face off, but Sasha interjected.

"Chill out, man. Y'all going draw the attention y'all really don't need, and trust me people are already clocking your moves rather you've noticed it or not." Sasha said. Her Malian accent mixed with the southern drawl she'd adapted from living in Memphis for so long always humored them. But they knew Sasha was right. They fought their paranoia daily. Neither of them were bold enough to admit that they both felt like they were being watched or followed at times. Tati and Genesis were young and wild, they were anything but dumb. They settled down after a minute-long stare off.

"Her bitch ass need to learn to take a fucking joke, then." Genesis said.

"You just have to get the final word, don't you." Tati said, rolling her eyes.

"And do." Genesis said.

"Darling stop it, let Tati live. You've triggered her enough don't you think." Sasha intervened.

Genesis looked at Tati as if she was seeing her for the first time. It occurred to her that Tati wasn't angry. She looked afraid. What Genesis believed to be a senseless joke was an actual worry for Tati. A part of her believed she may really be pregnant, and Tati didn't have the kind of heart that would allow her to abort her child, regardless of it being conceived out of scandal and deceit. Genesis swallowed her pride. She leaned over in her seat and hugged Tati.

"I'm sorry boo, I didn't mean to hurt your feelings." Genesis said, then kissed Tati' forehead. Tati embraced her back. She didn't say a word, but she accepted the apology and the love Genesis showed. It made her feel much better.

"That's right, hug that shit out. This ain't the bad girls club. We're a happy family in this piece." Sasha said. Tati and Genesis both looked at Sasha and laughed. Sasha was the backbone they didn't realize they needed.

"Where would we be without you Sash?" Tati asked with a kool-aid smile.

"Ah you see, that's a question only god knows the answer to." Sasha replied, coolly raising her shoulders.

Tati giggled. " You might be right, Sash. Well I'm going to leave y'all to it. I know y'all need your little alone time. And I gots to get some rest since we have big plans when day comes." She said.

"You are so thoughtful, when you wanna be." Genesis teased.

Tati scrunched her nose and threw Genesis the middle finger. Genesis caught it and blew a kiss. Tati kissed Sasha on the cheek.

"Goodnight love ones." Tati sang.

"Night Tati, sweet dreams." Sasha said.

Tati cupped her two hands over her heart and pursed her lips, a sign of thanks to Sasha' thoughtful remark, as she exited the kitchen.

Almost immediately, Genesis' shot Sasha the 'sex me' eyes. Sasha called Genesis' closer with her pointer finger. Genesis did all but drool as she lifted off her seat and obediently strutted her way into Sasha' lap. Their kiss was sloppy, they swapped spit like their life depended on it. Shasha smacked Genesis' ass so hard that it startled Tati from her bedroom. Tati sounded them out with some good ole Jill Scott. That was the only way Tati went to sleep most nights. Not only did Jill sound out unwanted noise, she also scared away the nightmares.
 Nevertheless, Sasha and Genesis got lost in each other's heat. The chemistry between the two was so electrifying that they got a rise out of every touch. Sasha slid Genesis baby blue lace shorts to the side and fingered her butthole while simultaneously strumming her clit. Genesis whimpered. Overwhelmed with pleasure. Sasha lifted Genesis to her waist as she stood and walked her to the bedroom.

Sasha slowly winded between Genesis' thighs as she gently laid her on the bed. Their tongues were intertwined as they tasted each other's lips. Genesis rubbed her hands through Sasha' waves. Sasha sucked her neck like she was out for blood.

"My sweet Isis." Sasha breathed into Genesis' ear. Isis was the nickname she gave Genesis. Genesis was the first book in the Bible. It was the beginning of the world for the Christian faith, but Sasha knew the history of ancient Egypt which said that Isis was the mother of humanity. The beginning of the world began through a woman. Sasha knew Genesis name was a play on that since the Bible duplicated many of ancient Egypt's philosophies. Genesis was pleased to know that even her name was connected to something royal and powerful.

Genesis helped Sasha unbutton her Ralph Lauren button shirt. Sasha wouldn't take off her wife beater. She never did, no matter how much Genesis encouraged her. Sasha still wasn't ready to reveal that part of herself. She had many battle scars and war wounds. Genesis would caress the wounds and kiss the scars that showed.

"Yeah you're always so wet for me baby." Sasha said. Genesis was dripping wet. Sasha was so turned on by it she began licking Genesis all over from her earlobes to the heels of her feet. Genesis was in a state euphoria. She didn't have to beg, there was no need to guide. Sasha knew exactly how to please her. Genesis purred. She opened her legs into a Japanese split as Sasha placed three fingers inside of her and mangled her clitrios like the juiciest mango. It felt so good that Genesis shedded tears. Pleasure shot through her body like a lightning bolt. Sasha alleviated her boxers and began to mesh her pussy into Genesis'. They were both wet. The sensation caused an immediate climax between. Sasha choked Genesis as she winded her hips at a fast pace. Genesis fingered her as she matched Sasha' rhythm. They came together and fell asleep with the bodies and sex juices intertwined.

***

At twilight. There was knocking at the door. Genesis was a light sleeper so the noise woke her at an instance. She tumbled out of bed to check to see who was at their door unannounced. She grabbed her pistol and proceeded to squint through the peephole. Her blood boiled at the sight of an unfamiliar woman standing on their doorstep.

"Who the fuck is this bitch?!" Genesis whispered.

Aaliyah had contemplated her visit to Tati and Genesis' apartment for hours. She knew there were great risks involved. Her life would be at stake if Tati and Genesis had an irrational response. Her career if her captain got word of her unwarranted visits. Her clothes were wrinkly and soiled from sitting in her car for nearly twelve hours. She had a severe hangover from all the Jack Daniels she'd drank over the course of a week.

Genesis swung open the door just as Aaliyah was about to knock again. Aaliyah rocked back and forth like a zombie. Her weave was matted and unkempt. Genesis thought she was a dope fiend who'd lost her way.

"Say miss, I don't know who your supplier is but you are at the wrong door." Genesis said.

Aaliyah tried to laugh but her mouth was too dry, it seemed more like she was trying to keep her teeth from falling out. Genesis frowned, disgusted. Aaliyah was unaware of her appearance, she'd been so engrossed in the investigation that she'd allowed her personal care to take the backseat. She was otherwise a beautiful woman with a well meaning heart, but her job had taken its toll on her. Genesis saw something in Aaliyah. It was something about her that caused her disgust towards the strange woman to turn to concern.

"Ma'am are you okay?" Genesis asked in spite of her guarded demeanor.

Aaliyah did that laugh that made her look toothless again, then caught herself.

"Genesis, right?" Aaliyah asked with her hand held out to be shaken.

Genesis zoned in on Aaaliyah' face. She walked so close to the woman that they were sharing one breath.

"Who the fuck are you?" Genesis asked coldly. Her tone was stern and deadly, but Aalyah was unphased. She was packing heat as well, and she was highly equipped to use it. Aaliyah leaned into Genesis' ear. Genesis wanted to vomit, because Aalyah' breath stank something terrible.

"You...called my...department...with...a..tip." Aaliyah whispered.

Genesis' eyes bulged. She backed off, and stepped into the apartment. Aaliyah stopped her from closing the door.

"You are not in trouble Genesis. You are my savior. I've been at these cases for years. Some of the children may be adults now, some may be dead. Whatever the case. All I am seeking is closure for everyone involved." Aaliyah said, she held Genesis' arm pleadingly.

She looked so pitiful from Genesis' view. Genesis could tell that the woman wasn't a harm to anyone, but herself. She wanted to give the poor lady closure. She could have easily put the unguarded woman out of her misery, but Genesis gut had told her this day would come. She believed that it would be a mother putting out a 'missing' poster for her child. Genesis had imagined she'd walk up to the grieving mother and bless her with life changing information. Although they had trashed the phone, Genesis had kept the SIM card and the SD card. Genesis left Aaliyah waiting outside the door. She stood in the living room in a state of shock. It was a cop right outside her door. A cop, who actually did her job. One that cared so much that she was deteriorating before her very eyes from her undying pursuit to solve cases the rest of the world deemed hopeless. That woman deserved a break. Literally and figuratively, she needed to rest. Genesis began to cry, silently. It'd seemed like a dream.

"Lady, I don't know who you are, but for some reason I trust you. And I ain't trying to be the one blocking you from bringing some children home to their families." Genesis said after she handed Aaliyah both the SIM card and the SD card.

" I'm Aaliyah Hopes, and yes that's my birth given name." Aaliyah said as she jittered and rocked.

Genesis nodded. She watched Aaliyah closely until their eyes made a clear connection. Genesis wanted Aaliyah to feel her from a place words couldn't express.

"I have nothing else to give you. This ends here." Genesis said.

Aaliyah nodded. She understood. Genesis didn't want to be contacted for any further questioning. Aaliyah leaving with those items of solid evidence was a contract. Aaliyah agreed. Tati and Genesis were not criminals, they were saviors.

***

Hours later, Genesis, Sasha, and Tati were out scouting buildings for sale. They were looking for the perfect spot to open their new nail salon.

Genesis had not discussed her encounter with Aaliyah Hopes. Genesis trusted Aaliyah to do the right thing. It was just something about her visit that told Genesis that God was stirring the pot.

The perfect spot. They agreed on this abandoned food market on the corner of Fifth street in Downtown North Memphis. The business would be called Black Queens Nail Bar. Tati and Genesis were so excited. They raved about how they would transform the old store into something beautiful. Sasha made a call to a close friend, who then appointed them a date and time when they would have an official tour of the property. They would decide if the property is worth the price and the work. If everything went smooth they would finalize a contract and the property would be theirs. Once Sasha saw the amount of money they came up on , she knew they had to clean it somehow. Starting a business was their best bet. They both agreed upon the nail shop. The near future was on the upside.

***

Tatiyana waited nervously on the edge of the bathtub. She bit her lip, anticipating the results on the stick. She'd been late for her period, and had an odd feeling in her belly. It could have just been paranoia , but she couldn't be sure. After days of worrying and procrastinating. Tati was prepared to accept motherhood, She wouldn't get rid of the baby if the results came out positive. Her nervousness had turned to hopefulness, but when she read the results it was negative. She eagerly ran from the bathroom.

"I'm not pregnant!" She yelled to Genesis and Sasha who sat on the couch watching Peaky Blinders.

Genesis smiled. " Congratulations, you whore. Now you can move on with your life and stop being a paranoid bitch." She said.

Tati hopped on Genesis lap and hugged her face to hers. " Aww, where would I be without you?" She asked. Sasha laughed at their interactions. They were very sarcastic with each other at times.

"On some real shit though, congratulations. You deserve to be free. We both do. We don't need to be tied down to that situation any longer. That shit is dead so let it die." Genesis said.

Tati hugged Genesis some more.

"This the G, I know. My mothafuckin bitch for life."

"And is."

***

Genesis Perspective

See not all black girls lost remain trapped in a life of despair and bitter rage. Some of them become queens. As much as the world wants to judge us. God has blessed us. We were witnesses to so many black girls becoming victims and slaves to the harsh hand they were dealt. Even though our families had abandoned us, the system failed us, and the streets tried to make our memory nothing but some teddy bears on a light pole, we strived and we survived. Yea, Yea. We survived through all that fucking chaos. Now we get to live. We got a booming operation with the Black Queens Nail Bar taking off and carving a lane of its own. We got money we ain't even touched yet. We up there if I must say so myself. I figured I'd gone travel the world for about a year, and let Tati hold down the village while I'm off playing, eating ,praying, and loving with my studsman Sasha. Don't trip my girl Tati is more than protected. Mookie never stopped looking out for us. She is our adopted sister. An added bonus to our allegiance. But anyways, I done shared too much already. I just thought y'all should know that these two queens survived the storms and did everything but walk on water to prove that God is real. Aight tho!

BLACK GIRLS ARE KINGS

By

Damita Taylor

"I raised myself I transformed myself and no one will lower my banner" - **Clara Nuñes**

"*Pussy niggas get dropped. You sucka niggas too flawed. Trick ass bitches, cowardly lions, y'all lack courage and the heart.*" -Egypt's verse.

"*...Ion travel first class cuz that shit just basic, I hop on jets, fuck up a check, then I ride yo nigga face...*" - Zion's verse.

"*On god!*" "*On god!*"

Egypt pushes a forest green Maybach Benz, seventy-five in a forty-five mile limit. Police sirens blare sporadically, racing behind the Black Kings. Krown who sits in the backseat smokes a fat blunt as she bobs her head rhythmically to the booming music. Zion hangs upside down out of the front passenger seat, throwing finger signs and pretending to bust shots at the police. An antsy cameraman sits next Krown recording all of the action. Bystanders spectate enthusiastically on the sidewalks and porches of the North Memphis hood that the Black Kings float through.

"*I am inciting a riot. You don't want no smoke, bitch chill. Quiet down, you talking that shit a real nigga like me don't feel.*" -Krown's verse.

"*On god!*" "*On god!*"

This could easily be real life, but this afternoon it is action on set. Black Kings are filming a visual for their latest record *On God*. The hood came out in droves to support the well known female rap trio.

In between takes, Egypt, Krown, and Zion sit in director chairs and watch retakes from the shoot. Zion holds her two year old son Cosmo as he sips juice from his baby shark sippy cup. Their fans snap pictures and lives for facebook and instagram to broadcast the starfilled action. Champion Knight, a young pretty journalist, approaches the Kings. She sits down in an extra chair that is provided by a production assistant.

They don't pay her presence much attention. Champion is humble and hungry. She doesn't appear intimidated by their brick-like demeanors at all.

"Black Kings, it's an honor to finally meet you beautiful women. I'm Champion Knight. A writer for the Infamous Minds digital magazine." Champion introduces herself with a million dollar smile and undeniable confidence. She watches for their acknowledgement of her. Cosmo giggles and happily kicks his feet. Champion waves respectfully at the bright toddler, but her focus quickly returns to the women before her. They aren't as engaging as she expected. She waits about a minute, assuming they are just that into the footage they are critiquing for their **On God** visual. Just when Champion stands insulted by their disregard of her mere existence, Egypt reaches out with a magnetic smile and shakes her hand.

"You are a patient lady, I like that." Egypt says.

Champion nods, pleasingly. "Thank you. I was beginning to think I was a peon trespassing on the step of you guys' star powered universe." She laughed at her own nervous joke.

Egypt hugs the shoulders of Krown and Zion. Zion shakes her hand graciously, then smiles down at her bouncing baby boy. Krown salutes Champion and winks.

"Nice to meet you, Champ." Krown says.

Champion smiles. "That's dope I've already made it to nickname basis." She says. Then, she effortlessly prepares her interview materials. She hooks a wireless mic up to her iphone, which she connects to her digital camera. The vibe was much better.

"It's no secret that you all are the new wave of radicals for our time, but that is not always well received by corporations who'd otherwise lend their sponsorship. However and remarkably so you women have maximized a brand that challenges the tradition of business and marketing structure. How does it feel to be the epitome of a force to reckon with?" Champion asks.

Egypt, Krown, Zion and even Cosmo look at each other, appalled. Egypt, the more outspoken of the group busts out laughing.

"Damn mane, you studied the thesaurus to the tee huh sis?" Egypt asks.

Champion smirks. She knew her statement was far too wordy, but she had to get her point across.

"Sorry." Champion says.

"Nah, don't say sorry. I respect that. You put a lot of thought into us. I could tell." Zion says.

Champion nods gratefully.

"And to answer your question. We never focused on building a brand. The whole intention behind our artistry is to be ourselves no matter who feels a way. We radicals for sure, but the brand comes from us being educated and studying the game." Zion says.

Krown continues, "When you remain true to your voice and what you stand for, the money gon follow. You know what I'm saying. Energy is a currency all on its own."

Egypt nods in agreement. "That's right. Self made, well paid. Does that answer your question Akeylah and the bee?" She asks mockingly.

Champion smiles bashfully. " Yeah you guys are great."

"Next question." Egypt says checking her Rollie.

"Many will argue that you women are attempting to neutralize your place in a male dominant industry by calling yourselves kings. Why do you choose to title yourselves Black Kings when y'all are such exceptional black queens?" Champion asks.

That question riles them up. Egypt sniffs at her agitation. Krown shakes her head coyly. While Zion sits at attention. They are quiet for quite a while, making Champion second guess herself once again.

"Did I say something wrong?" Champion asks apologetically.

"You too soft." Egypt says, candidly.

Champion frowns defensively. "I'm not soft. Who do you think you are?" She asks.

"I am Egypt Moore, a young black millionaire who came from the dirt. I really live the shit I rap. I really survived wars, and I'm not talking about Vietnam."

Champion shrugs nervously. Egypt has the glare of a made killer. Her rawness is provocative. Krown chuckles.

"Chill Gypsy. Don't give her a hard time. She's just doing her job." Krown says.

"She needs to cut that soft shit out. Stop apologizing. The fuck is you sorry for anyway?" Egypt asks, with sincere concern.

Champion shrugs. Her feelings are hurt. Cosmo starts to whimper. His lip quivers with sadness. Zion rocks him with a motherly embrace.

"We are not a gimmick. Black women are Kings, because we rule humanity. A queen comes at the side of a king. A king stands at the head of the throne. The throne is life. We are the heads of our lives. We are limitless and we are the greatest rulers on this earth under God." Zion proclaims. Cosmo comfortably snuggles into her bosom.

"Facts." Krown says with finality.

The Black Kings' hold a posture of high esteem and total self awareness. They are each beautiful in their own unique way. Their individual personalities set them apart in a highly distinguished way. Egypt has soft features that contradicts her hardened personality. Her eyelashes are full and dark. She has soft curly hair that flows down her back with a neck full of tattoos. Her style is slightly boyish, but her femininity is fierce. Krown has stronger features, nice succulent lips, piercings on each of her wide nostrils. Thick Baby blue hair. Zion is chocolate with soft long hair. Her style is unapologetically sexy and feminine. A sexy trio of women who carried themselves with dominance and certainty. Black Kings.

Champion sits inspired. She doesn't want to leave them. They have a refreshing energy that she's been missing. She wants to be a part of the history they are making. She begins to see Egypt's rudeness as a bluntness to provoke her betterment. She arrived to do a quick artist profile for her column in versatility and cultural influence, but she now sees an opportunity to maximize history in the making, through her lens. Without any manipulation only uncorrupted observation.

She makes an effort to cease the opportunity, "I would like to do a documentary on you kings. An interview isn't enough for the depth I intend to capture. I want to be the voice in the media that gets it right."

"What are you saying? You wanna follow us around like the goddamn feds?" Egypt blasts her.

"More like a guardian angel, but with a camera." Champion says with certainty.

Egypt squints at her critically. Krown and Zion are both thoughtful.

Champion continues to sell her proposal, " They won't be able to Michael Jackson you. They won't get to tarnish the legacy you've founded." Egypt clasps her hands together like a mob boss, and leans back in her chair. Champion's words ring nice in her ears.
Zion smiles and kisses her son. " I like you, Champ. Stick around girl cause we gon' take you some places."

Chapter II
The wedding bells ring on the shore of a beautiful island resort in Cuba. Krown and her husband -to-be Murk stand at a shrine of flowers and offerings of well wishes. Egypt is Murk's best man. They have been friends since elementary. She's been like a brother to him his whole life. Especially after his brothers were murdered a year apart his ninth and tenth grade year in high school. Zion stands at Krown's side. Their mothers and a select few of their closest loved ones are in attendance. Champion captures the moment with her camera. The waves push back and forth offshore. The view is enchanting. The light of the sun makes a runway across the sparkling turquoise sea.

The priest reads Psalms forty-five and anoints their heads with oil. He welcomes their loved ones and says a prayer of thanksgiving. The soft breeze sways Krown's knee length cream satin dress. Murk keeps it player in his silk blouse and trousers. The priest asks anyone who objects to speak now or forever hold their peace. No one speaks. He prompts the couple to go ahead with their personal vows. Krown gazes into Murk's eyes like she sees heaven in him.

" I was always your secret admirer. From the very first day I saw you, your smile made me feel at ease. I was a nervous wreck, before I met you. I think about the day in that alleyway often. If it wasn't for you I'd probably be in prison right now. But instead I'm here with you, the love of my life. My soulmate. Thank you Murk, for being far more than a lover, you've been my most trusted counselor, this is just the icing on a cake that's already sweet without it." Krown tells Murk as they stand hand in hand. She places the wedding band on his marriage finger.

Murk begins, " I knew you was good for me from day one. Not only was you sexy, you was smart, and independent. You carried yourself with respect and that caught my attention. It didn't take long for me to fall in love cause I trusted you with my whole heart. You a real one bae and you haven't failed me yet. Loving you is the easiest and dopest shit I ever done. And now I get to call you my wife. God is smiling on a nigga no doubt. I respect and honor you, my Krown." Murk finishes his vows and uses Krown' fist to wipe his tears. He places the wedding band on Krown' finger and kisses her hand. Egypt pats his back encouraging him, that it is okay to show his real emotion. The priest pronounces them husband and wife, and gives them permission to kiss before the applauding crowd. The doves are released from the cages. The wedding singer serenades the newlyweds with Anita Baker Sweet Love.

The reception is nothing short of an enjoyable time. They dance near the water and enjoy food from a private chef. Champion lets loose a little and twerk to a few songs. The liquor has everyone on a high key vibe. The mamas are even dancing. The newlyweds cut their cake. The bride tosses her bouquet, and Champion races to catch it. Egypt does not let her live down the moment. She teases her nonstop about it. Champion just laughs it off and keeps it moving. Friends and family share encouraging words over the newlyweds. The night is one for the books. The love shown is immeasurable.

'God Bless'
"I come from a ghetto with a bad murder rate, seen niggas lose they life over materials I dare you to take, and it's a lesson learned to get my jewels insured, cuz I can't be too sure if I'm ready to die or take a prison tour over a few hunnid K. I went from running up granny' pressure, to sitting in Empress' tesla, talking deals and avenues to keep that wealth consistent. Now the whole team running up major digits,. This wasn't always the intention. Murk is here Krown is here they know my whole beginning. They hold my darkest secrets. It brought my heart some peace to see they love prevail, cause I remember Krown was ready to throw her life to jail cause niggas wouldn't let her live. I look back on our childhood selves, and shed a few gangsta tears. We in Cuba on an island , and I'm proud of us. Last night was wild as fuck. I rode a Cuban nigga' face like this what I grinded for. He gripped my thighs some tough and sucked all my juices up. I went to sleep and had a dream I was with Assata Shakur, she spoke some game and told me it was time for change. Thought I saw Pac. I did, he had a

wife and kid, but maybe I'm trippin cause henny and weed bring out that rebel energy...America ain't what it seems, government don't want us free...and I'm affected by the poison, how you take a man from his daughter? Another caged bird with broken wings still we all got choices and we all got voices..."

Egypt woke up inspired to make music. Although they were tired Krown and Zion sat with their pens and pads adding their verses to the thirty-two Egypt had already laid. Champion filmed them and captured still shots of the young women in action.

Krown added an auto tune melody for the hook. "God bless, all of the hopes and dreams I had. I made it out the jungle. I'm rich, fly out to islands for vacation. The last of the real, we made it, yea we made it, God bless."

"I booked seven wins off the cards I was dealt, blood sweat and tears, prayed to the Heavenly Father that he take away these pretty little fears, cause this girl here, ain't have a father figure to lean upon, momma and granny was my only confidantes. Cosmo my only son, he makes momma smile. He my reason to thrive and Black Kings gon' forever strive, these my niggas no question we in *this shit together, I'mma always ride. Black is pride, I had to set my pain aside in order to organize this lavish life."* -Zion's verse.

Egypt leaked an early release of the song. The record achieved massive success on several streaming services. Their guerilla style methods towards creating and releasing music on their own terms challenged the dynamics of traditional labels. It was aggressive and highly effective, which gained them both positive and negative exposure.

Egypt throws a lowkey kickback with Zion, Champion, and Krown. Champion grows closer to them day by day. They each have their own separate bonds with her. She is always there to listen and help them make sense of things, especially when it comes to the media's antics, and the way they are portrayed. They are playing a game of billiards. Their latest album booms through the surround system. A Los Angeles Sparks vs. The New York Liberty game plays on mute on the mounted smart screen. They puff cigars and sip whiskey like they are at a classic country club. Annoyed, Egypt scrolls through her phone.

She goes on a slight rant, "Mane fool, who the fuck keep reporting our shit? Everytime I repost somebody showing love to the single the shit gets stripped down. The fuck is going on mane?"

" You hurt a lot of feelings with that verse, Gypsy. But you knew it would be pushback when you chose to release the shit." Krown replies.

"Yeah girl, that comes with the politics of the game. People don't like to hear niggas talk that revolutionary shit, but you know this." Zion says.

Champion films their conversation, she never intervenes verbally unless they suggest her input. She listens, intending to bring a cinematic feel to the reality of their circumstance. Zion blows chalk from the tip of her billiard stick and attempts to shoot a ball into the hole from an awkward angle. Needless to say she misses her aim. Krown and Egypt are too immersed in the conversation to notice the miss, so she steals another go.

"But that shit not affecting the bread so it shouldn't matter. The people have spoken, the song is fire, to hell with the hating ass corporations." Krown says.

"That shit goes against my constitutional rights, though mane. I'm not tryna hear non of that."

"Aight now, W.E.B. Du Bois." Krown teases.

Everyone laughs. The doorbell rings, then comes an alert from the security monitor. A middle aged black male dressed in a secret service type suit awaits them. Everyone is frozen with apprehension. They are spooked by the unforeseen presence at their friend's home.

"That's the fucking feds, y'all." Egypt says.

"How the fuck do he know where you stay?" Krown asks.

"I don't know, but lemme gon face this demon." Egypt says.

Zion and Krown are terrified, but they trail behind her. The man is taller than he appeared on camera. He looks down at them nonchalantly. The encounter is quick.

"Egypt Moore, you've been subpoenaed by the federal bureau investigation." The man handed Egypt the envelope and made a robotic-like exit.

The Black Kings were stunned. The FBI had gotten involved due to Egypt's remarks about Assata

Shakur who is listed as a FBI most wanted terrorist. The FBI enforced Egypt to revise her lyrics or else she would be indicted for creating terrorist implications. They couldn't believe that they were receiving that extreme amount of pushback for one verse. Krown and Zion advised Egypt to put her pride aside and take the loss, but Egypt refused. Instead Egypt went against the grain, and started a live instagram post. She spoke defiantly against the powers that be. Her fans fed into it. They were just as angry as her. They conspired a petition to the Supreme Court to uphold Egypt's first Amendment rights.

" America ain't gon never change if we keep letting these blood suckers control our culture. This is art. I'm painting a picture with words. How they gon try to silence me? I'm a young black woman, I'm a king bruh. How they gon try and stop the only thing that saved my life? If it wasn't for this music shit I'll be in the goddamn penitentiary. They already took my daddy from me. My mama gone off that dope, till this day we don't speak. So I'm asking who the fuck are they to tell me what I can and can't say?"

Zion and Krown sat in the shadows. They understood Egypt's message. It was her approach that unsettled them. Egypt was untamed and fearless. She felt that the people needed to be made aware of the injustice going on.

"I'll be a lie to say I don't want y'all to ride for me, but if y'all don't then shit I'll just face this shit by my muhfuckin self."

The comments on Instagram live were going crazy. She had her audience full support. She started a movement, and gained Black Kings a different lane of fanfare. Egypt's live went viral. It was being shown all over social media. Every post got thousands of shares. Zion and Krown didn't appreciate the heavy exposure. They made an attempt to counsel her.

"Gypsy, baby girl. You know we're gonna ride for you regardless. Right and wrong. But you gotta see the forest for the trees. Even if you don't change the lyrics, that's cool. But you're summoning an energy that I don't think you ready for." Zion said with pleading eyes.

"Yeah, Gypsy. This shit is bringing on drama that we don't need. You know they gon' try to tear you down in other ways if they can't silence you the way they want to." Krown added.

Egypt was quiet. She pondered around their advice. She concluded that they are acting out of fear. Her mentor Empress Black helped earn her a master's degree on the ins and outs of the music industry. She couldn't process why Zion and Krown were acting so politically correct. First off, they were independent artists. They were not industry slaves to any label. They were owners and competitors up against major labels. She realized that they were afraid that something may happen to her, like many greats who went against the status quo and challenged the masses to think. Egypt assured them that she was different. She let it be known that she was ready for war, but she was also gung ho on prevailing and staying true. It was a situation they had to agree to disagree on, but either way they had to keep moving forward.

Chapter III
Champion's Perspective

I always knew the day would come. I'd seen it happen to so many great artists before their time. The Black Kings had founded a platform that was so autonomous and rare that it was bound to intimidate the business models of larger companies. They had overthrown an outdated structure.

Egypt had said nothing wrong in her rap. She wasn't inciting terrorist influence. She was simply voicing a dream and expressing her ideas. The FBI was a bully tactic sent by hidden powers to silence her. Egypt was fearless. They all were. Zion and Krown were not afraid of controversy. Their whole career went against societal norms. They just didn't want the drama to overshadow what they had built. They didn't want to become a gimmick. They were young legends who understood their impact on the game. I empathized with them. Before anything I was a true fan of their grind and their artistry. When I first came on board my intention was to document their everyday lives, so they wouldn't need any media outsource to distort their narrative for profit. They were the masters of their destiny and it was my job to assist with that without them even realizing it.

***

"Mane this is a dream come true. I remember I used to look up at the sky and imagine this shit." Egypt was like a child at DisneyLand for the first time. I loved to capture those moments of Egypt. She had an innocence to her that wasn't always recognized, but I could tell from the very start. Egypt didn't have much of a childhood. Murico Moore was incarcerated since she was six years old. He was serving a double life sentence for felonious drug trafficking and homicide. Egypt was a daddy's girl to the core, she kept in contact with him faithfully. It's like she held on to those special moments they spent before his sentencing. It brought her so much joy to be able to relive one of those special moments, by putting on a block party and free concert in the neighborhood where she grew up. She was a spitting image of him in almost every way, but I soon learned that she often channeled her father's style and mannerisms as a way of keeping his name alive. Her father's persona often revealed itself in two ways: through her anger and through her performances. She smiled at the frame and I captured it. It was a beautiful picture. I could tell she was smiling from her heart. It was a win for the child inside of her. Krown hugged Egypt's neck and kissed her jaw, like the big sis she was. Egypt was younger than Krown and Zion by three years. I photographed the intimacy of the moment. Their intentions were pure. Nothing was for show.

"I'm happy for you boo." Krown said.

What I loved most about my methods toward journalism was that I needed no extra glamour or pretend grit in order to sauce things up. The Black Kings were a journalist dream. Every move they made was genuine. Sometimes imperfect, offensive, sexy, fly, or simply human. Whatever the situation was, they never asked me to cut or edit moments out. At times I think they forgot I was even there. Cosmo attracted a lot of the young ladies in attendance. Zion allowed his massive afro to breathe instead of his usual braided designs. The young ladies raved about how adorable Cosmo was. Zion let him charm them with his cheeky smile and cute baby talk. I enjoyed Zion's admiration for her son and his way of engaging with others. He was a little magnet of fun and joy. Murk played the background mostly. He watched them like a proud and protective father.

The various free vendors of cotton candy, funnel cakes, barbecue plates, nachos, and other tasty treats for the youth were set up nicely along the rec center curbside. There were cool activities like a shot clock shooting game, an enormous bouncing house, they funded the city bikes and scooters so that youth could freely ride throughout the community with unlimited time. There were all types of contests and giveaways. Black Kings had invested a lot in their free event. It was a fun time for everyone. The concert was my favorite part of course. I knew every word, and I loved to capture creative angles of their individual stage presences. It was like a music video in live action. The crowd was into every word. A Black Kings concert was nothing short of lit and upbeat energy. Those women knew how to move a crowd. They performed three of their latest bangers: On God, God Bless, and Bitches Be Like. They'd made their stamp. The crowd was impressed and appreciative of the excellent performance and hospitality they received.

As we were approaching our sprinter a young man yelled out for Egypt. He jogged up to the van. Krown, Murk, Cosmo, and Zion had already settled in. I stood at the door with Egypt right behind me. Everything happened so fast. The man was dressed in flashy designer clothes with bukoo chains. I assumed he was an aspiring rapper. "Baby girl, lemme holla at you." He slowly reached behind the inside of his denim vest. Egypt's smile quickly vanished. Without any hesitation she whipped out her pistol and started firing. I screamed and fell to the ground.

Egypt helped me to my feet and we jumped into the sprinter. Cosmo was crying horrifically. Nobody else knew what was going on. "Drive motherfucker, drive. That was a goddamn set up!" Egypt said to the driver. We sped off from the scene.

The media had a field day with their distorted take on the story. They connected the story to Egypt's past involvement with gangs. Even though Egypt had been inactive since she was sixteen. The media twisted the story to make it seem like The Black Kings were in the neighborhood stirring up chaos, but the whole event was peaceful up until Egypt was approached by the strange dude. I had to speak up. I released a mini documentary of the entire event, including the moments leading up to the event to showcase the hardwork and dedication that went into making the block party and free concert a success. The true supporters spoke out in droves. They combated all of the mainstream gossip sites and made corrective posts on Egypt's behalf.

Zion's home, I learned, was a safe haven for the Black Kings. She shared a home with her mother and grandmother. Zion still had her childhood bedroom. Everyone was shaken up by the shooting and really needed to recharge and close out the rest of the world. Ms. Zeal made a delicious homemade meal and even more scrumptious dessert. It was a wholesome family affair. We sat around the dining table eating and just enjoying each other's company. I learned something about the ladies almost everyday. Still, I had yet to ask the question.

"How did you all meet?"

"Krown and me been cool since ye high. Even though she was three years older we ran with the same folks. We ended up in a halfway house for runaways and at risk girls. That's how we met Z." Egypt answered.

"Yea we were all on the same wave. We rapped and just used to kick it." Krown added.

Zion nodded her agreement to their statements. I had wondered how they made their connection. I knew Krown and Egypt came from the hood, a very crime ridden hood might I add. But Zion had come from an upper class upbringing. Her mother was a therapist with an independent practice. I didn't see her connection to the streets.
"If you don't mind me asking, Zion how did you—"

Zion interrupted me before I could finish the question. "I was a runaway. I went through a phase, that's all."

"Yes she did, but it was very necessary so that she'd find her own way." Ms. Zeal said.

"Yea I think we smothered her with so much love that she needed to branch out into the world in order to make her tougher." Zillion said.

"Thanks momma." Zion said.

Zillion winked at her with a smile. She fed Cosmo peach cobbler and ice cream. The thing that stood out to me most was that although their strength and poise was admirable, the lack of male presence in each of their lives had impacted them negatively at some point in time. They all had to heal from that void. We laughed about childhood memories they shared and happy memories they had created throughout their career. Ms. Zeal wanted to know a lot about my background. It was a little awkward being that I was used to observing and asking the questions. The spotlight made me a bit uncomfortable.

I informed her I was originally from Clarksdale Mississippi. I moved to Memphis at eighteen to attend University of Memphis. Soon after I graduated, I received my masters in journalism from University of Southern California. Now at twenty-five years old I used my platform as a journalist to maintain the legacy and integrity of three women I thought the world of. I was the youngest of four children. My parents were already in their forties and fifties when I was born. I was real down home, southern, and just mild mannered, but I was raised on integrity. Ms. Zeal was more than satisfied with my explanation.

"You are a fine young lady, Champion. I can tell you come from good people. I appreciated that story you put out about my grandchild and her friends here. We are all really one big family, you know." Ms. Zeal said.

I smiled gracefully. I felt I'd done a job well done. If Ms. Zeal had gotten the purpose of the story, then there was no way the media could distort the Black Kings' image any further.

Chapter IV
As soon as Egypt floated her classic blue stingray corvette into her driveway she was surrounded by policemen with guns drawn, the sirens and blue lights startled her and caused her heart to race. She slowly raised her hands showing surrender. The police snatched her from the car and slang her on the ground, cuffing her wrists in an instance.

Egypt paces the floor of the single person cell. She's been processed for four hours and hasn't taken a seat yet. She cannot find comfort in her predicament, pacing the floor allows her to feel a little empowered in her situation. The muscles in her feet and calves are burning and aching but she does not give in. A buzzer sounds. Keys jangle. The metal door slides open.

"You've posted bail Miss Moore." The jailer says. An air of relief comes over her. He hands her a bag to change back into her personal clothes. Minutes later she meets the light of the sun.

Egypt is expecting to see Krown and Zion. Instead she is met by Empress Black leaning on the side of a black Maybach. Egypt did a double take before running to hug Empress. Empress is Egypt's mentor. She is the mother Egypt never had.

"Empress, lady what are you doing here? I didn't expect to see you."

"It is long overdue. We've been out of touch for too long and it shows."

"Let's get out of here though."

Empress and Egypt cruise around the city. Egypt munches down a cheeseburger and fries. Traffic is heavy, but they are in no rush so Empress drives slow while sipping a strawberry lemonade. It's about eighty-five degrees out, but the maybach is nice, cool and comfy. Empress is patient, allowing Egypt to finish up her food. Egypt knew whenever her and Empress linked wisdom was going to be shared. Empress let Egypt rock, she didn't interfere often, but she did intervene when she felt Egypt was getting out of hand.

"I know from the outside looking in shit seem like it's going bad for me." Egypt says.

"That may be true if I didn't know you. I practically raised you Gypsy. I see what's going on, but I'm here to make sure you are good. Is your mind right? Is your spirit healthy?"

"I didn't get in the game for this. I got strangers speaking on my name. A nigga tried to take my life, but these folks surrounding my crib like I'm a villain. They know it was self defense. I was at my own event, why the fuck would I kill a nigga just because? This shit is all by design. They do it to all the greats. As soon as a nigga show these white folks that we ain't gonna play a slave, a crackhead, or a fool with gold they try to defame our name somehow and when that shit don't work they lock us up, and when that don't work they try to kill us."

Empress lets the heat of Egypt's words warm the car. They sit in silence, neither of them are too eager to speak. Empress has been a part of Egypt's life since Egypt was sixteen. She met Egypt at her darkest-lowest time. Egypt was so immersed in the street life that she would lurk the streets until dawn high off percocets and possessed by inner demons. At any moment Egypt was ready to kill or be killed. Her earlier raps and freestyles were about constant murder and hatred towards rival cliques and gangs. Empress was nonjudgmental and compassionate toward Egypt when she was least receptive but needed it the most. Empress had heard a viral freestyle of Egypt's and went directly to her hood to connect with her. Though it took some time, Empress took Egypt under her wing and helped her get on the straight and narrow.

"That verse is monumental, people will look back and see that you were coming from the sincerest place possible. How iconic you were, because a little black child with so many odds against her not only survived them, but you became a superstar and then on top of that you educated yourself and aligned with your history. You are an icon, Gypsy baby."

To Empress surprise Egypt's head was bowed, like a defeated little girl. Tears dropped onto her exposed thighs.

"And if I'm all of that, why do I feel like my whole world is slipping from my grip?"

"Because, baby girl, all God's chosen have Judas. My father's first born son was his. To hell with the press, Gypsy baby everything will be fine"

Empress lifted Egypt's head with the point of her manicured nail just like she'd done for her younger brother many times before. She wiped the tears from Egypt's face and hugged her with so much love all Egypt could do was surrender and sigh.

***

Two months later. Egypt has been on house arrest since the day after her release from county jail. The crew has been at her crib recording, vibing, and doing their best to remain in good spirits. They are in Egypt's home recording studio, tripping off the classic film Set It Off.

"If they ever make a remake we gotta play that shit. It'll be perfect I'm telling y'all." Krown says as she pastes together the slim blunt with her lips. One blunt is already in rotation, but when they are in creative mode one blunt is never enough between them.

"Facts, but who gone be who tho?" Egypt asks with the most relaxed grin.

"Zion is Stoney for sho, I'm Frankie, Gypsy you would play the fuck out Cleo role, and Chmapion ass gon be Tee-Tee." Krown says.

"Damn why I gotta be Tee-Tee for?" Champion asked, her eyes are low as an elderly Korean woman' as she sits in the cut recording them behind the camera.

They all burst out laughing. "Bitch that is why." They say as one, then burst out laughing some more. Champion opens her mouth like she is appalled, but joins in on the laughter.

"I guess it makes sense, shit. Tee-Tee wasn't so bad though." Champion says.

Egypt's phone rings. A photograph of her childhood self and her father pops on the screen.

"Aw shit. It's Pops y'all."

"What up Pops!!" They all sing into the phone. Since her house arrest, Egypts has been taking calls from her father in prison more often.

"What's going on, young niggas?!" Murico's voice echoes on speakerphone.

"We in the studio Pops."

Murico laughs , " Is that right, lemme hear that fye." He says.

They play a snippet of a newly recorded track they laid hours before. Murico is so amped up by the cadence and flow that he begins rapping over it on impulse. His energy is electrifying. Krown presses record on the engineering board just in time to capture the last sixteen bars. He is breathing hard and ranting on by time the beat fades out. Egypt cries tears of joy. Finally she will be on a record with her father's infamous lyrical presence.

" I think we just made history daddy." Egypt beams with stars in her eyes.

Champion smiles a tearful smile. The Black Kings take a tug at her heart string for the untenth time, and she does not resist the powerful emotion. She is simply grateful to be a documentarian of such moments.

"Ayyee, you the better version of me. I'm just happy to be around to see it." Murico words have much pride.

"Daddy we gotta get you on more tracks. You done started some shit, my nigga."

" Haha, ayyee that way young nigga."

"I love you Pops."

"We love you Pops."

"I love y'all folks too mane, keep y'all foot on they necks. Y'all on they ass for sho."

The call ends. The girls all bug out dapping each other up and yeeking with excitement.

"That man ate that muhfuggin song." Krown says.

"On me. We got some shit coming for sho. Topnotch Rico. The fucking legend. " Zion gloats.

The girls reactions are so pure a Topnotch Rico verse to them is what a feature from Jay-Z would mean to most rappers. They make plans to use that exact conversation as a soundbite for the intro of their upcoming surprise album.

Three a.m. rolls around, the ladies are still in the studio now tuned in to an Ava Duvernay documentary called 13th. Murk enters the studio with bags of takeout. By now they are sluggish and drowsy, watching the mounted flatscreen with red eyes and growling bellies.

"I know y'all fools got the munchies. Here go y'all food, now hand over my wife." He says.

Krown smiles tiredly. "Coming baby."

"Yea that's what I like to hear, now bring your ass girl."

"Boy calm down. You act like I neglect your ass or something." Krown replies as she hugs and kisses all the ladies goodnight. Murk smacks her on the booty as they exit the studio. Egypt smiles, it still amazed her that two of her closest friends had become lovers.

***

It took six months for the jury and prosecutor to deliberate a verdict. Thanks to the greatest attorney at law as her representation and the undeniable evidence, Egypt was found not guilty and acquitted of all charges. Based on the evidence of self defense.

Award show night, a celebratory vibe is rampart in the air. The women decided to wear velvet smooth tailored dresses. Egypt's dress was black, Krown's was red, and Zion's was gold. Murk and Cosmo rocked tuxedos of the same velvet material. Murk matched his wife, while Cosmo matched his beautiful mother. Black Kings were nominated for several Panthers, which was an award trophy by the Black Supremacy Music Awards.

"Wow ladies, we are getting a never before seen look tonight aren't we? The Black Kings are surely goddesses in the flesh. Stunning I tell you." A beautiful middle aged reporter showered the ladies with compliments as they stood on the black carpet attending the press release. The ladies cordially thanked the reporter. They were no fans of compliments and flattery, plus the press had never been their best supporters.

"What can we expect from your performance tonight, Kings?"

"The same as always, raw, untamed, and fierce energy." Zion answered for them. She was the unspoken spokesperson for them in times of discomfort and in the face of fake love.

"Wonderful. You ladies are up for quite a few nominations. How does it feel in spite of all the negativity attached to your brand these days?"

"We ain't no fucking brand, and I don't know which news you been watching but the real life I'm living show us taking back to back wins and receiving hella love." Egypt spoke up.

"Oh sorry I didn't mean to offend you."

"You didn't, did you?" The Black Kings turned their backs , avoiding any more press. Zion and Krown comforted Egypt.

"Enjoy your night ladies, have a great show." The reporters well wishes fell on deaf ears.

The Black Kings posed for pictures and headed into the ballroom for the ceremony. Their performance was well received by the audience. They won three of the seven nominations. After the show they happily pose with their trophies.

Empress hosts an award show afterparty at her night club lounge EST. 1992. She honors Black Kings and a host of other winners and nominees of the night's awards. The Black Kings are in their element mingling with peers and supporters.

The elegant and upper echelon decorum is extravagant enough to compete with traditional affairs such as the Grammys or the Academy Awards. Empress takes no shortcuts and shoots for the most distinguished quality when it comes to her ceremonies and affairs. Interactive slideshows of historical black figures such as Sir Black Sr, Muhammad Ali, Malcom X, Shirley Chilsom, Harriet Tubman, Madame CJ Walker, Eartha Kitt, Whitney Houston, dark skin Michael Jackson, and so many more are engraved into the brick walls. Treasure boxes of jewelry and ancient African statues such as the Black Madonna, King Tut, Isis and Osiris, Black Christ, etc. are posted in every corner. The furniture from the tables to the sofas and chairs are made of natural wood, leather, and top level fur. The color scheme is jet black and crystal white. The floors are made of authentic quartz crystals. The decorum is an ode to the foundation her father's legacy stood upon. The menu of the finest shrimp and chicken pasta, salad, top shelf wine, pastries, multiple chicken wing flavors, and collard greens are assorted on a stylized table against the wall.

Empress takes to the stage. Sending the night away with a powerful message, " Thank each and every last one of you for your contribution to this night and the overall business of music and entertainment. It is not often that we are celebrated in our rightful deservance. Our counterparts do often tolerate us by giving us partial inclusion into their institutions of ceremony. However, we have and will continue to be the blueprint for culture, influence, and style. We must not place our bets into spaces and places that are not designed for our nature. We must trust our own and uplift ourselves. We are not victims nor are we second class citizens, and if that is hard for you to believe at least let your contributions to this industry be your reminder..."
The audience gives a thunderous round of applause. A very special night for all in attendance.

Moments later, Empress and the Black Kings sat inside her Wrath smoking cigars and vibing to Anita Baker. Empress gifted them all solid gold Rolex watches. They flashed their new collection into Egypt's Instagram live. Champion captures the moment from a cinematic view with her camera. It was a moment for them to be young and free. No worries, no responsibility.

"Shoutout to big sis, good looking out!" Zion sang into the camera phone.

Their fans were just as happy as they were. It was such a good time that Egypt spontaneously accepted a fan's request into the live. When she accepted the request the screen was facing the ceiling.

Egypt joked, "Oh you wanna show off ceilings that's what we doing?" She said and showed the stars inside the wrath.

"Fuck you man-hating bitch. It's death to your on the low dike ass. Count your days bitch, because it's bounties on you." An unidentified male voice raged through the phone.

They froze in shock. Egypt felt violated. "Nigga do you know who the fuck I am? I'll find you myself and get the job. The fuck you hiding for coward ass fuck nigga?" Egypt pressed him right back. The male disconnected from the live.

"We need to get the police involved ASAP." Champion said in an instance."

"Shut it off." Empress instructed. Egypt reluctantly took heed. Their eyes met with a shared concern.

"We can't afford to take no threats loosely." Krown said. "We gotta beef up security." She added.

"Nah fuck that. I'm war ready. Ain't no nigga finna chump me into hiring no fucking bodyguards." Egypt said nonchalantly.

"Gypsy! Put your pride to the side for once and just listen to us. We can't afford to take chances on your life sweetie. This is nonnegotiable." Zion yelled full of terror, her heart raced fast.

Egypt quietly sat back with her legs crossed. Her voice cracked as she spoke, " I'd rather die than live my life as a scared ass slave."

"Empress, please talk some sense into your girl, because how I'm feeling right now. I could slap her." Zion spat.

Egypt glared at her. " Who stopping you?" She challenged Zion.

Zion dismissed her by putting her hand in the air. "Girl bye I wouldn't give you the satisfaction."

"That's what I thought." Egypt chuckled.

Empress sat silently. She trembled with unbound anger. The self entitled fool who'd threatened her beloved mentee brought on bitter memories of her father's demise. Another undeserving coward had the audacity to invade their celebratory moment with threats to their life. Empress wasn't going to allow that. She ransacked her brain for the best possible solution. Her only hope was that someone had screen recorded that live.

***

Almost immediately, Empress made arrangements for Egypt to move into her Miami mansion. Egypt, being Egypt, tried to put up a fight but Empress wouldn't take no for an answer. Within days they were on a private flight to Miami.

Miami was the getaway Egypt hadn't known she needed. She lounged outdoors by the pool most nights, blowing loud, and listening to her father's verses he'd made from the prison calls. During the days she needed her father more than she ever had, she spoke to him the least. She didn't wanna bother him with her troubles, since there was nothing he could do about it. Egypt was not fearful for her life, however she felt powerless and guideless. For the first time in years, she was without Zion, Murk, and Krown. She was reminded that she was an only child. She'd made her friends her family along the way, but her father was the only blood relative she knew to call. Empress went overboard. She had her most trusted men secure the premises. It didn't matter to her that Egypt felt that the troll's threats were idle, she'd seen proven suckers make good on those threats many times over. She wasn't taking any risks with the young woman she'd taken under her wing. Egypt was the baby sister she'd never had, and she would've guarded her with her life if the need surfaced. Egypt didn't leave the house much. Throughout the day, she stayed in gaming, eating by the caseload, and watching an unbelievable amount of conspiracy movies and documentaries. Empress advised her to fast away from social media until things digressed.

Empress phoned for Egypt to meet her in the conference room. Empress abided. Once downstairs, Egypt was met with Empress and her assistant looking over a platero of paperwork and itinerary. Egypt was clothed in a red Land of the Trill short set. Empress scanned through contracts, but without looking up she sensed Egypt's hesitance.

"Have a seat, Gypsy. We need to talk." Empress said.

Egypt abided, "What's going on, E?"

Empress took a sip from her coffee mug, then stared at Egypt. "I'm taking a month-long trip to Europe. I have a few developments to settle, and I want you to come with me."

"Nah. No, I'm good where I'm at. I'm not going no further than this, E."

"You're too comfortable being comfortable. It's only a month Gypsy. You'll learn so much from this trip. I'm meeting with some really dope independent artists overseas. It'll be good networking."

"Nah I'm good on them peppa pig sounding fuckers over there."

"See there you go with that close minded mindset. I told you about that girl. You can't knock something you never tried."

"I don't wanna try, E. I wanna be left on."

"Suit yourself, I won't pressure you, but I will have eyes and ears on you while I'm away so don't get no slick ideas, Gypsy."

"Okay, mom. Damn."

"You got that right. You are the closest thing to a daughter I'll ever have. Lock that in your big knucklehead, punk."

Egypt smiled menacingly. "I'm gon' throw a wild ass party while you gone, watch."

"Gypsy, you got way more important shit to prioritize than a silly ass party."

"I'm just playing damn."

Empress stared at Egypt a little too long for comfort. Egypt shrugged and looked off at the horizon that seeped through the sheer drapes. "Yea and while you're playing it's somebody out there scheming on your life."

Egypt sucked her teeth and glared at her bawled fist. "I'm not worried."

"You aren't worried, but you should be Gypsy."

"For what ? It don't change nothing. I'm going against myself as it is. Hiding out in a city that's not mine. I'm ready to get back to M-town. I been here long enough. "

Empress slammed her laptop screen shut. She breathed in deeply as she took a long sip of her coffee. She didn't want to say any regretful remarks. She needed her intention to be clear and understood. Egypt stared off into the beautiful beach horizon, fuming and afflicted with pride.
"Egypt you are an adult. I can't control your decisions. I can only trust that I've instilled in you enough wisdom to guide you through this storm. It will pass, but I want you to understand I'm doing this out of love. I don't wanna lose you to a senseless act of violence. But if you have to leave

and you feel that's what's best I will respect your wishes and keep you in my prayers."

Egypt walked over and hugged Empress tight. "I love you, E. I won't let you down. I promise."

"I love you more Gypsy baby."Empress kissed Egypt's cheek, and quickly caught the tear that streamed down her face.

Two nights later, Empress had left for her trip to Europe. She would be gone for a month. Egypt had the mansion all to herself with watchmen posted in their respective assigned posts throughout the estate. Empress lounged in the game room playing Grand Theft Auto 7 on Playstation 4. She sipped her chocolate-brownie milkshake and munched down a turkey sandwich made by the in-house chef. A couple hours into eating and gaming, Egypt fell asleep with milkshake slobbering down her mouth.

A man with skin is black as coal entered the room like a slithering thief in the night. The sclera of his eyes were as yellow as toxic piss. He smoked the stankiest-thickest cigar one had never seen. He was about six-foot. He wore a suit red as blood and a green fedora. He sat next to Egypt with the

200

familiarity of a father. His ice cold presence awakened her in an instance. She snatched her glock 40 from under the gaming chair and aimed it at his dome ready to let the fire sing, but the man displayed no fear. He was silent and thoughtful. You'd think she had invaded his personal territory instead of him invading hers. Egypt tried to speak but her tongue was entangled by the grip of an unknown force.

"You may die..." The man's voice was thunderous enough to awaken and disrupt the waves of the sea.

Egypt frowned in paralyzing terror. The man patted her knee. He smiled and his hard triangular dimples stretched toward his ears. He was a demon in the flesh. The time on the sleeping screen read 3:33 am. Egypt recalled a time her granny told her that three o'clock was a demon' hour. She shuddered at the realization.

"Don't worry, because it does not stop at death. You see Gypsy baby, there are worlds, schools and even scientists have not warned you about." He chuckled, sat in a chilling silence savoring the aftertaste of his enormous stinky cigar.

Egypt could not speak, yet her question echoed inside her head. " What do you want from me? Who let you in here?"

"I am of the spirit world baby chile, don't you see. I tread without borders." He replied aloud.

Egypt was stunned but happy to be heard. "What do you want from me?" her mind echoed again.

The man was silent and still as a brick. He faded into the darkness then emerged again, his presence was colder than thirty below weather in the wintertime. Egypt shivered, but could not physically move her body. He grinned sinisterly at her helplessness.

"Gimme yo soul, Gypsy baby. Lend it to me for just a little while. Gimme your soul and you'll have access to worlds you never could have dreamed." He roared a horrific laughter.

Egypt jolted awake, panting and sweating bullets. It was all a dream, still terror quaked within. Her heart fluttered sporadically. She went downstairs to the kitchen to fetch a glass of water. The mansion was so spacious and grand, even if there was a house full it was still lonely and too quiet for Egypt. She sat at the counter and facetimed Champion.

Champion connected on the third ring. She was lying beneath a comfy blanket, her head wrapped in an African printed scarf. She and Egypt stared at each for a moment, wordlessly.

Then, "I'm not alone." Champion said.

Egypt nodded. Champion turned the camera facing Zion with Cosmo asleep right next to her. They were in Zion's family living room.

"I had a bad dream, Champ."

Champion pursed her lips with sympathy. "You did?"

Egypt was still shaken up by it. Her voice trembled as she said, " The devil asked for my soul."

"Oh baby, that is scary. That's some dark shit."

"I feel like my time is near, you know what I'm saying. I feel like I won't be here for long."

"Gypsy, baby don't. Don't talk like that."

"Gypsy?" Zion asked. "You're on the phone with my sister, and you weren't going to say nothing? Wow." Zion snuggled into the loveseat that Champion occupied. Champion and Egypt exchanged a look.

"What up, Zion?"

"I missed you stranger."

"I missed y'all more. I'ma be home soon, though."

"When it's safe, Gypsy." Zion said.

"I'm not worried about safety. It's necessary for me to be home in my city. This shit unnatural."

Champion and Zion laughed.

"You so damn hard headed, oohwee." Zion said.

"I'll touch down in a few days."

"We'll be at the airport waiting on you, baby."

Everyone knew there was no arguing with Egypt once her mind was made up, plus they all missed her anyways.

***

Against security protocol Black Kings attended a function with a gang of other black creatives and young entrepreneurs who were mainly from Egypt's and Krown childhood community. They were excited to reunite with people they once modeled their lives after. The event was at a local nail salon, called Black Queen's Nail Bar. Women were in the majority, but men were there to collaborate and show their support as well. It felt like old times. They danced, laughed, played a few unreleased tracks, copped merchandise, and simply had a good time. Tatiyana, the co-owner of the nail bar, approached them for a photo op.

"Y'all know what's wild. I knew y'all lil hoes when y'all was just some pups, now y'all the real big dawgs, and that's facts. I'm so proud of y'all right now." Tatiyana said.

Krown and Egypt laughed happily and hugged Tatiyana. It was always a pleasure running into the ghosts of the past. Tatiyana was a living legend.

"Tati what it do, love. It's been a minute." Krown said as they embraced a few seconds longer.

"I told you I was a superstar. You ain't wanna believe me." Egypt said playfully, like she was delivering an inside joke.

"I told your lil bad ass to stop running around the streets acting like a goddamn demon, because I saw your potential. So don't play Gypsy." Tatiyana said. Egypt dapped her up. Tati stood between all three of them and hugged them once more, as Champion captured the photo.

A crowd had formed surrounding the storefront. It was the time of night when the hood ballers liked to show their expensive toys. It was a beautiful time. Various car models from old school cutlass supreme, box chevys, cameros, Corvettes with suicide doors, mustangs, Rovers, Benzes, porches, chargers, and cadillacs. Egypt hopped in her forest green Maybach. A hired security guard posted in the front passenger seat. Krown, Champion, and Zion trailed behind her in Krown's platinum rover. She was in such a good mood. She turned on a song her father had written for her as a child.

She my sunshine on a cloudy day, she drive my pain away. She made a man of me. I ain't never looked to God this hard before, I got another chance. You know I been scarred before. And I ain't perfect by a long shot, I broke some hearts before. She my love child, a sweet redemption, my second chance to get right. I hope my baby don't suffer in this life, cause mistakes her daddy done made to earn his stripes. All that real nigga shit go out the window, I shed tears of joy the first time I held you. You was so pure, simply beautiful. I tried to marry your momma but daddy brought the queen too much pain and drama, silly dilemmas I let interrupt my family, and I ain't proud of the different levels I failed you, but I know you forgive me everyday you smile at me. I guard you with my whole heart, you the piece that was missing you my whole heart. My sunshine on a cloudy day...

They were in such bliss. Enjoying the fruits of their labor, but there is always a sweet and subtle calm before the storm. The shots rang out like grenades. Eight shots darted into the car. The maybach swerved and tumbled over. It all fades to black for Egypt. She instantly fell unconscious. Tatiyana was the closest and first to run to her aid. She struggled, but succeeded in getting Egypt out of the car, before it set to flames.

"Relax Gypsy baby. You gotta relax." Tatiyanna's voice trembled as the bodyguard struggled to make out what had just happened to the 911 operator. Krown, Zion, and Champion encircled Egypt in a disarray. Screaming, crying, stunned by the whole situation. The crowd was in a frenzy, running for cover. Some spectated the scene at a close but respective distance.

Amiss the media mayhem. Krown, Empress, Zion, Murk, and Champion sit at Egypt's bedside. She is hooked to several tubes, and is not breathing on her own at the moment. They are prayerful and look to the comatose loved one with hope.

"I failed you, Gypsy baby. I'm so sorry." Empress says then sobs uncontrollably. Her cries ignite a room full of tears. They all feel a sense of guilt and failure. Unbeknownst to them, a major part of the world mourns with them. Strangers who've only known Egypt through music and interviews root for her recovery. Although there are many rumors circulating about set up and betrayal, their only focus right now is to see their sister pull through.

It has been five days and still no sign of recovery for Egypt. Murk and Krown decide to make a store run to finally get everyone something to eat and refresh themselves. Security is all but connected at their hips. As they wait for their order to be done at the Chinese spot, Krown and Murk make a trip to the nearby gas station and buy four pregnancy tests. The store clerk congratulates them.

"Welp I take it you two are expecting a positive outcome, no one buys that many tests unless they already know the answer. Congratulations beautiful people." He says. They smile exhaustedly and dryly thank him.

Inside Egypt's hospital room. No one has an appetite. They barely touch their food. Their eyes ache and burn from all the tears they've cried. Murk sleeps with his head at Egypt's feet, while Krown hides out in the bathroom awaiting the results of the third pregnancy test. Just as the first two, the tests come back positive, but she has nothing but time on her hands so she takes the fourth one.

The doctor enters the room along with the registered nurse. The doctor explains to them that they will have to perform an emergency procedure on Egypt.

They advise everyone to leave, except Empress, who has the power of attorney.

"What? No, we can't just leave her." Zion speaks with such an exhaustion that the doctor and nurse pity her.

"Everything will be fine. I got her." Empress says with great certainty.

The doctor smiles, sincerely. Although his face is pale, and they've adapted a mentality to never trust his kind, he has sincere energy.

"We'll give you all the time you need. The procedure won't be performed until tomorrow morning." The doctor speaks sympathetically and exits the room with the nurse at his heels.

Zion massages Egypt's hand. "I don't wanna leave her. I'm scared I might miss something." Her voice is easy from crying and the lack of sleep.

"Cosmo need you, Zion. Empress going to keep us updated. I trust her. And you know Gypsy a fighter. We gon come out of this on top." Murk says kneeling at Egypt's feet as if his words are a prayer he hopes God hears.

"That's right. Our Gypsy is a fighter." Champion says with a hopeful smile as she watches Egypt with deep endearment.

Zion kisses Egypt's hands. Champion kisses her forehead, Murk kisses her covered feet. Although they'd rather stay. They know it is best they leave and trust that everything will be alright. Empress loves Egypt like a daughter or a baby sister. Egypt literally had entrusted her with her life. They couldn't argue with that.

"Baby! Are you good?" Murks asks, tapping the bathroom door. Krown doesn't answer, so he makes his way in. She's sitting on the toilet with the saddest face.

"What's wrong baby?" Murk asks as he swats to meet her daze.

"I'm pregnant, Murk."

"That's a good thing. Baby I'm gon' be somebody's daddy."

"Why it gotta happen like this? Why do I gotta lose my sister right when I'm bringing life into this world?" Krown cries.

Murk is thoughtful. Krown words are heavy and spark fear into him. "We ain't lost her yet, baby. We can't give up on Gyspy. Gypsy strong, so we gon be strong. We having a healthy baby and we gon ride this thing out to Gyspy back to herself again. No matter how long it takes. "

They all depart the hospital, leaving Empress by her lonesome to watch over Egypt. She promises to keep them updated, and they promise to get themselves some rest and not to hassle her.

Chapter V

Zeal cooks comfort food. Shepherd's pie, mac and cheese, yams, collard greens, and fried chicken. Krown, Murk, and Champion sit at the table with Zion, her mother, son, and grandmother. They bow their heads before the wholesome meal, for grace and thanksgiving. The food smells and tastes delicious. The mood is quite somber. Smooth jazz resounds throughout the house. Silverware clicks and clacks against the plates. Zillion's phone rings. She apologetically excuses herself from the table expecting it to be work related. She returns from the call drenched in sorrow.

"Gypsy didn't make it. She passed away an hour ago."

They were so exhausted, so defeated, that all they could do was lower their head and shed silent tears. It was out of their control. The feeling of grief was not new, but life without Egypt would be a mountain that they may never fully climb. Egypt was the warrior, she was the strength. Without her voice, her input, nothing felt right. There was nothing to be said.

The national reports of Egypt's passing causes an uproar from the fans. News footage shows fans in the streets bawling their eyes out and raging for Egypt's justice. Black Kings' music sales skyrockets higher than ever before. Fans blast their songs throughout communities across America. They finally see the full impact their music has had on the world. Although they are mourning, Krown and Zion can't help but be proud. Champion releases an official documentary "Black Girls Are

Kings" based on their life story and experiences in the industry. The documentary tugs at the heartstrings of so many. Clothing that depicts their imagery is monetized. Fans began tatting Egypt's, Krown, and Zion' faces on their bodies. Their stardom rises to a new stratosphere.

***

Egypt's Perspective
When you are a superstar, death is an investment. I knew my group was too hot on the radar. I was the blame, so I did what I had to do to make things right. One day soon I'll send them a sign to let them know that I'm alive, but for now it's peaceful. They're mourning for the Egypt that no longer exists. I had to dead her and reinvent myself. Empress mapped it all out. The threats were real, but her adamacy to keep me alive and untouched wasn't to be played with. I wish I could break it all down. But the clues was there from the jump. I'm in a villa on an island I can't disclose. My pops was in on it. I began writing to him in my pseudonym months ago. I gave him clues and he peeped game. My people are suffering, but they're getting richer. I'll fill them in soon, because you either play the game or let the game play you. So just call me the muhfuggin most valuable player!

Flowers In The Concrete

By

Damita Taylor

I've seen the beauty in everything but me. I saw God in everything but myself. Why can't I love myself? What makes me consistently go against myself? I've adapted the curse of unworthiness. No matter what I've accomplished I continue to be unsatisfied with me. The state of my existence seems so unbelonging. I've loved so many only for them to never know how I truly felt. I have lived my whole life being misunderstood. And it's all because I have never understood myself.

I am awake before the birds sing their new day song. The sun has not cracked a slit into the sky. The moon is ever fading but still shares its glowing light. I made a personal vow to be productive today. I don't flip on How to Get away With Murder and toss two breakfast sandwiches in the microwave like usual. Today I boil water, and rinse my favorite mug. As I sip my sweetened ginger tea, the cup tells me to commit to the Lord whatever I do and my plans will succeed. A gift from my beautiful God fearing Auntie Tricie. Aloud I recite affirmations I wrote last night:

"I forgive myself for the harm I have caused to myself and others."

"I give myself permission to begin a new start."

"Yesterday is no more. Today is a blank canvas, I will create the picture I want to see."

"I won't do drugs today. I won't do drugs today. I won't do drugs—."

I can't finish the last affirmation. The thought is attached to too many overwhelming emotions and desires. I become woozy, then I am compelled to quit before I even start. But I will not quit. I will try my hardest, but for now, today I'll take baby steps. As long as the steps are a step forward from the mistakes I made yesterday. Yesterday I didn't speak affirmations. I wouldn't have dared tried to spell away the urge of my favorite candy. I would have set my alarm thirty minutes before my class time, and rushed out of the door with a mouthful of breakfast and sleep half washed from my eyes. Today is progress. I make it a chore to drink the entire cup of ginger tea, then I scramble for clothes comfortable enough to take my early morning bicycle ride. It has been ages since I rode my ten speed Trek. It's been picking up dust in my closet for months now. I throw on grey biker shorts, a red Nike sports bra, and an old pair of red Nike

Huarache sneakers. The sun stretches its light throughout the purplish sky. I set the timer on my watch for thirty minutes. The goal is to complete 10 miles there and back in that timeframe. My path begins at Powers Road down Jones street, and up and through Austin Peay Highway. I cycle without music, because I read somewhere that addictive behaviors derive from the constant need of motivation from sources outside of one's self. I allow my anxieties to run rapport. Sweating, heart racing at a mile a minute. I constantly look over my shoulder, but I can't say for certain if it's reasonable cautiousness or irrational paranoia. The fatigue hits me in a matter of minutes, but I will not stop. I ache through the distance, my thighs feel as though they are locking. I think my heart is on fire, but I keep on going. Multiple men in various cars honk their horns at me like I'm a trick-turner off Lamar Ave. "Piss of shit, fuck boy." This is my range of thinking. Those men infuriate me. Talk about road rage. I feel that I may collapse. Maybe I've set the bar too high. I should have eased into such a rigorous workout. Mind over matter. By the time I make it back to Powers road, I am so overcome with dizziness and muscle failure that I collapse to the ground vomiting out my insides.

"Yaya what's wrong?" Aja, my twelve year old neighbor asks me. She has it made up in her mind that we are best friends. I go along with it because Aja has kept many of my humiliating secrets. The child doesn't miss a beat, and she holds water so well I'm surprised she doesn't get sea sick. I clasp at the concrete for dear life. I vomit to the point that I become dehydrated. I gasp for air and clutch my breast.

"Oh Lord, let me get granny, before this girl dies." Aja says then flies into her complex. She returns with Ms. Mabel and a mason jar of ice water.

"See grandma, look at her. She never works out, why today Yaya? What's so different about today?"

"Aja leave the girl alone, don't you see she's suffering enough without all your criticizing."

"Yes ma'am. Here you go, Yaya."Aja hands me the water and rubs my back. I gulp down the ice cold water gratefully. It stirs a funny feeling in my empty stomach that causes me to gag. Yaya and Ms. Mabel look at me with pity all in their eyes.

"I'm okay, guys. Don't worry, this is just a result of my relentless effort to finish what I started."

"Your huh?"

"You heard the girl she's okay, this is what happens when your body says stop but you keep on going anyhow."

"Yeah, oh."

It's 5:45 am. There's no telling why Mabel and Aja are up, but with these two it could be anything. I live a floor up from them in a small tight-knit apartment complex. Majority women and children and a few quiet mild-mannered men. I've known them for three years now.

"Thank you so much Ms. Mabel, and Aja you are such a gem, sweetie thank you for coming to my rescue."

"Aw shucks, that's what friends are for, Yaya. I'll always be there for you."

I smile, Aja is an adorable charismatic little girl. If I was to have a child I'd want her to be as dope as her. Ms. Mabel looks from me to Aja and chuckles heartily.

" I love to see it, I tell ya." She says, then she helps me to my feet with Aja's assistance. They invite me to breakfast. Turns out Aja has a full day ahead of her. She is visiting her incarcerated mother today right after her interview with a highly prestigious STEM program for the summer. I wish her luck, and respectfully decline the breakfast invite. Maybe next time, I assure them. Before I head off to class I wash away my vomit from the sidewalk with pine sol and hot water.

***

I am a law student in the final stages of my Thesis. I am revisiting the trial of Hannah Abdullah v. Tennessee. Hannah Abdullah was an Islamic street artist that used her art to make political statements across the city of Memphis in 2007. Muhammad argued that her art was a form of expression protected by her first amendment rights. The state prosecuted Muhammad because it was a crime to vandalize public and private property without proper permission from the city or its owners. Muhammad became more radical in her plight. She began marking school buildings, churches, and local government buildings. Muhammad was sentenced to forty years to life. As I revisit the trial, I delve deeper into the evidence and its contents. I come to the conclusion that Muhammad was wrongfully convicted. I have already completed the historical context. I presented the facts and clauses. I have implemented many constitutional rights and their meanings. Muhammad had broken zero laws. She'd only ruffled a lot of powerful feathers. I had reviewed the trial records. I learned that Muhammad's lawyer was a conflict of interest. He was a former prosecutor, but became a defense attorney after a disappointing political run. His opening argument was extremely loaded and misleading. He spoke so casually on Islamic terrorist groups and their vendetta against America. I found that to be a strike against Muhammad, especially when he failed to follow up with a stronger counter argument against his formal statements. The defense used the bias as a weapon and railroaded Muhammad mercilessly. I was floored, and knew that Muhammad deserved an appeal, rightfully so. I was prepared to do the work.

In my Lawyering Seminar III class, the professor picked each of our brains and checked to see where we stood as many of us reached the finalization of our thesis. I explained the conclusion I had reached, and told him the possible methods I would utilize to bring out a successful outcome. He appeared pleased, informed us of a new deadline, and dismissed us. I never stay on campus too long. Most of my studies take place online. The professors appoint meetings ever so often to maintain some mutual respect and interest.

***

I have recently taken on a job as a public defender. It allows me to gain field experience while pursuing a law degree. My days get extremely hectic. I represent ten to fifteen clients at a time. I aim to give each of them their proper just due, but most times I fall short.

"I'm not coping no fucking plea. I was not there at the time they trying to say the nigga was robbed. I was at my momma house." My latest client Deante Ross, is a self entitled lawless menace. He lacks the funds that would compensate me and the courts, however he wants a Gotti style trial, it makes my ass itch when I'm handed these kinds of people. He is a bold face lie. There are witnesses, liable witnesses that are ready to pinpoint him as the suspect they witnessed arriving and fleeing the crime scene.

"If you cop a plea, you'll be out of prison by the time you turn twenty-eight. If you fight this it's a chance y'all be incarcerated well into your fifties."

"Say what?! Hell no, the devil is a motherfucking lie. I wanna fight this. They don't have no hard evidence proving that I was on the scene. Like I said I got my alibi."

"And you know this to be fact based on what actual proof?"

"I was at my momma's house. Shit. How many times do I gotta tell you?"

"Mr. Ross, you are gambling with your life here son. I'm giving you the best that I got in exchange for the crumbs I've been given. A trial takes money and time. And the more time the trial takes the more money you'll need, and it's unfortunate yes, but you can't afford this gamble you're taking."

Deante drops his defeated head. I'm relieved to see the glimpse of surrender in his eyes. Four years is what he'll be sentenced to with the plea deal. That's the best that I can do. A small price to pay for a young man who doesn't even know that there is a huge chance of video footage of him at the crime scene being presented at trial. At his hearing he pleads guilty and is arrested right away.

***

College friends become family. Mercedes, Angela, and Chanel are my sisters. We all moved back to Memphis on a mission to invoke change and to be pillars of our communities instead of turning our backs on it. Mercedes is a high school Algebra teacher. Angela went from working for the postal company to becoming the youngest City Secretary in Memphis' history. Chanel is just Chanel. She's a hustler and she wears many hats.

"I just don't understand it. Maybe it's the effect of the social media era, niggas want me ready and made easy like I'm something to just pop in the microwave at his disposal." Chanel is up in arms about another failed situationship.

"It does get tricky because it's the illusion we are all being fed. The average man can make a few posts about the ideal desires and fantasies a woman may possess, and if he posts enough decent pictures he's sure to attract 20% of those girls. Not to mention the women he encounters in everyday passing. Now put that same theory in reverse as it pertains to women and what to do you have?" Mercedes presents us with her statistical theory.

"A bunch of niggas and bitches with too many options to choose from." Chanel says.

"I don't know. I think more people are lonelier than they are willing to admit and most relationships aren't all that sweet. I mean people go through it just to maintain a level of comfort and public imagery." I say.

"I don't give a fuck. Point me to the real niggas, where them endangered species at?" Chanel says.

"Girl, you are a trip." Mercedes says.

"She's a whole fucking comedian is what she is." Angela says.

"I'm serious, I don't want no fake love. I want some real genuine, 90's R&B type of love and affection, do y'all hear me?"

"Yes Chanel, we feel you." I say.

"But you don't hear me though."

"We hear you sis, trust me." I assure her.

"I hear you, but I gave up on that fairytale romance bullshit the movies sell to us women. I get the dick

226

in the way that I want it, at any time that I want, and that is alright with me." Angela says.

"Do you care about diseases?" I ask.

"Or soul ties?" Chanel wonders aloud.

"Bitch I care about this lil' cat getting her itch scratched, I go to my check ups faithfully. I'm good. I don't do dirty community dick, just afraid to commit dick." Angela says unapologetically.

I'm always quiet on the topic of dick. Yuck. I can't relate to desiring a man in that way. I crave the affection and intimacy of a woman. A woman's touch is firm and soft. Her lips are like wondrous clouds. I crave a woman's curves, her complete feminine energy. The sweetness of her scent, and her nurturing silky voice. Yes I love women, but my sisters wouldn't relate. That's why I keep my line of discussion general, I don't go into grave detail much. We sip on wine and enjoy a delicious chicken fettuccine pasta and salad made by Angela. Whenever we link up there is always a big discussion or debate on some current social or political view. It is a habit we've formed from our undergraduate days. Angela is content with simply having a piece of a man, Chanel wants her ghetto knight and shining armor in the cloth of a real nigga, and Mercedes and I are focusing our energy into ourselves mostly, understanding that when it is meant to pass the troublesome linger of loneliness will pass. We sat around the oval shaped living room and tuned in to Michelle Obama's Becoming documentary.

"The world wasn't perfect, but it just felt different when the Obama's were in office. I didn't worry as much as I do now." Mercedes says.

"Yeah it was good for the psyche to see those beautiful black people in office." Angela says.

"Barack Obama gon' be my president forever, fuck orange chicken." Chanel says. Chanel never fails at making us crack up in laughter. Her care free attitude is the product of getting hers from the ground up with little to no support. Sometimes she just said what we were all thinking but too afraid to say out loud.

"Yea well, we have our two mini Michelle Obama's right here. Angela is our future mayor, and Yaya will be an extraordinary lawyer. I'm sure of it." Mercedes says.

"Thanks girl." I say.

"Yeah, mayor sounds good next to my name. Mayor Angela Thomas."

"That's right, my bitches are full of black excellence. A city ho could never." Chanel sends us to the floor laughing. Sis is a piece of work. My girls keep me in good spirits. They know that I have issues maintaining an upbeat mood, but they don't know I have an addiction. I function well, or maybe I put on a good show.

***

I sit at my study desk conducting research on the best way to move forward with obtaining an appeal for Hannah Muhammad. I can't help but become so bitterly enraged by the many wrongful and unlawful convictions of black women. I struggle to find the silver lining, but I know that these injustices have led me to pursue a career in law. I must trust my abilities, and I must enforce the law where there is a lack thereof.

I won't blame the travesties of others. I will not fault the world for being ungodly. I am in an ever need to escape the dark clouds that smother my mind. The clouds they surround me, and rob me of any inkling of hope. I can never pinpoint the cause, and I no longer make excuses. Because I don't know why I feel this way. I often ask why, but the question is unanswerable. I can only fantasize about a world of inner peace. Until then my candies call my name. They offer me a place of temporary refuge. Here I come, I tell them. However, tonight I don't want a temporary refuge. I want a high that lasts me until eternity. I cry for the pain to leave my body or to let me leave. I swallow pill after pill after pill. Until the bottle is empty and my brain is floating on a smooth sail of nothingness. I am nothing. I feel nothing. Let this be forever, let me be here forever.

Maybe it was the immediate neglect I experienced in my childhood. To have a mother and a father in the home, but still be no one's pride me joy. No one's eyes lit up when I smiled. No one urged to love me when I needed a hug. I used to stare out the window imagining a happy home. Where the mother dances and sings, and the father makes the best steaks and shows off his woman and child. No I didn't want to be a trophy, but I needed to be someone's happiness. I should have been celebrated. Why couldn't they see the light dimming inside of me? I should have been more outspoken. They say people only treat the way you allow them to. I should have never been so complacent. I was too trusting, I expected them to know how to love me. But I should have demanded them and taught them by the way I loved myself. I should have been prouder. More fierce. Instead I waited and waited, only to grow into an adult but still be inflicted by the voids of childhood traumas. No one's to blame anymore. I just figured maybe that's where it started. Everything went dark, and I surrendered. Maybe that's what heaven is. Sweet surrender. No fear. No attachments. Still no matter how hard I try. The feeling never lasts. I open my eyes and instantly feel pain. Physical aching pain. I'm so sore I cannot move. The bright light blinds me. My vision is blurry.

"You've always been a sad child." That is my mother's voice. I haven't spoken to her in a year. I haven't seen her since I graduated undergrad.

"Ma, is that you? Where am I?" I ask, my voice cracks from dryness and pain.

"You're in the hospital. They're going to run a lot of tests on your brain. See what's got you sick."

"No, I'm fine. Get me out of here."

"You've been comatose for eight days. The poor little neighbor girl alerted her grandmother after you were unresponsive to the knock at your door even though your car had been parked most of the day."

My sweet Aja. I'm starting to think she's my assigned angel.

"She saved my life."

"Yea, but you might have ruined hers. She thought that she'd lost her best friend."

As you can tell. There is not a lot of love and warmth between my mother and I. I've felt more compassion from strangers than I've felt from my own mother. Instead of consoling me at a time such as this, she scolds me.

"You can leave now, ma. I'll be okay from here."

"No you won't. You're a suicidal addict. The amount of Percocet found in your system was unbelievable. You're an abuser. The doctor had not prescribed you that drug." She sounds like a fucking snitch. Someone please get this rat out of my sight. Geesh.

"You never been there for me before now, and I don't need you now. Keep your judgment and leave on the high horse you rode in on."

"You're always ungrateful. Look at you. Blessed with beauty and you waste it with a woman. Blessed with two loving and devoted parents and you reward them by making their house feel like a living hell. You have intelligence. A bright future, but what do you do? You throw it all away by becoming a junky. Well if it's the devil in you telling me I've better leave, I'm going to save myself some trouble and listen."

"Yea ma, get the fuck out." My mother acted as if her presence was a favor to me. It was her need for a nut that brought me into the world, but I can only assume my father was the only one who came in that situation.

***

My sisters came bearing food, my favorite snacks, gifts, and their full support. I would be in the hospital for another three days until the psychiatrist and the physician felt that I was stable enough to discharge.

"Yaya I'm so sorry I couldn't see that you were hurting. I just thought you were overworked from school and that shitty job."

"It's okay Cedie. I kept my pain a secret because I was ashamed. You couldn't have known."

"But we call ourselves your sisters, Yaya. I'm sure the signs were there, we just weren't paying you enough attention."

"Us black women wear pain so well we just chalk it up as a part of who we are."

"Omg, Angie, you just said a mouthful. Don't we though?"

"I'm just glad we get a second chance to make things right. I don't know what I would have done if we lost you." Mercedes says then bursts into tears. We all console her. With these girls I feel the warmth. I know there is love.

"I love you guys so much. It means the world to me to have you all in my corner."

"We all we got baby girl. This is our fight now."

"Facts, we're gonna get you the help that you need, Yaya."

As if it couldn't get anymore cheesier, Mercedes began to sing "we are a family" from Dreamgirls. I loved every minute of it.

***

If you have a loved one who is inflicted by the dark clouds, you must know that they cannot help it. The clouds come unannounced and go when they please. We may push you away, because even the love you attempt to give causes us to feel worse. We may shun you, lash out at you, we may go silent and isolate ourselves for days at a time, but just bear with us. The darkness of the clouds makes everything hurt, especially the light you attempt to lend.

"Yaya, I'm only trying to help."

"I don't need help. I just need to be left alone."

"But you haven't come out of your room in days. I cooked food. You need a hot bath, the bubbles and epsom salt will make you feel better. You can't just wallow in your pain, friend. Come on."

"Mercedes, please. I know you are trying to help, but right now. I need to be left alone. I can't eat. I can't move. All I can do is lay here."

"I'm calling Ang and Chanel. This is ridiculous. You going to get your ass out of this bed. Even if we have to drag you."

Yep that's exactly what they did. Angela and Chanel barged into my complex like the fucking Avengers, yelled at me like they were my drill sargents, and dragged me out of the bed. They unclothed me and placed me into the bath Mercedes had so kindly prepared. I cried like an idiot. I felt far too detached from myself. My cry was so hollow and bitter, that they comforted me as they bathed me like I was some helpless being. Well, I was. I was helpless.

"Baby, you gotta go to therapy. I know a bad ass sister who does the work. She'll be perfect for you." Chanel said.

"I need my candy." I replied.

"Candy? What in the hell?"

"She's out of it y'all, we have to be patient."

236

"My percs. Can one of you get them for me?"

I think that was the moment they knew how down bad I was. They were quiet, saddened, and at that moment they felt helpless. My sisters realized that there was nothing they could do to truly help me. But that didn't stop them, they were relentless women. You know, black women are resilient creatures.

***

Zillion Moor House of Therapy. The garden in the front yard was really neat. The fresh scent of tomato and basil herb dazzled the air. Mercedes, Angela, and Chanel had all come with me to my first therapy session for moral support.

"Welcome beautiful people." Dr. Moor greeted us before we could even knock. She held the door open with a bright warm smile. The colors inside of the home were gorgeous. Vibrant and positive. Reds, yellows, greens, orange. Black and browns. We sat in the lounge area, where she offered us an assortment of pastries and tea.

"What brings you ladies to the house of therapy?"

"This one right here, she needs help. A lot of help."

"Okay, Chanel dang. She got it."Chanel smacks her lips. Mercedes has really been my voice these past few weeks. She's researched manic depression and it's root causes. She does her best to empathize with me when the clouds arrive. And when Ang and Chanel get frustrated with me Mercedes stays patient. Truth be told though, they were all sick of my shit. And I didn't blame them.

"You must be Yaya?"

"I am, and I'm an addict. I'm a recently diagnosed bipolar."

"I see, and I can tell that you've recently come to term with those truths."

"Yes, that's the first step to healing right?"

"Yes, Yaya, yes it is. But elaborate. What does being an addict mean to you?"

"Everyday I have a choice between life or death. Some days I don't know the difference between the two. My only goal is to escape, to free myself from the pain, or become so numb that I watch the pain as it hovers over me like it is waiting for me to return from my emotionless coma."

"You're quite observant of your disease. You seem to place yourself in the objective seat, although the addiction doesn't occur without your participation. When did you notice this addiction?"

"I had a friend who used to do acid. I used to join in but I always experienced bad trips. I didn't like the journeys and the long endurance of mind boggling visions. I needed something lowkey, an antidepressant. She put me on to percs. I loved the feeling, until I couldn't go a day without them. My tolerance got higher and higher. I'd pop up to twelve a day. It's been two years now, you know time flies. It seems like yesterday."

"Excuse me, What? I mean, Yaya, we have known you for four years. I never once noticed." Angela interjected. I could see the hurt of betrayal on each of their faces. But they shouldn't have felt betrayed. I hid my addiction out of shame. I didn't want them to feel responsible for that part of me, because they weren't.

"Right cause yea, who was this friend?" Chanel probed.

"An ex. It was some things I just had to keep to myself. I'm sure I don't know every little thing about you guys either." I said.

"Yea but it's not about us. And it's not like any of us are hiding those kinds of secrets from each other. You're an addict. We've found this out weeks ago, but you've been suffering for two years. That makes us feel a way Yaya. Don't dismiss us as if this isn't an issue." Angela said.

"Well what better times than now, ladies? In Yaya's defense a lot of shame is associated with addiction. A lot of times addicts don't want to be pitied or looked down on because of their addiction. Secrecy and addiction usually go hand in hand." Dr. Moor informed them.

"I don't mean no harm doc, but it's that type of enabling mentality that produce victims. This girl know we wouldn't have judged her. We don't judge her about anything she does. If anything, if she would have come to us sooner we would have got her straight. Just like we introduced her to you. The top therapist in the city."

"Take it personal if you want to Chanel, but this has nothing to do with you. It never has. I went through my depression way before I met you. Pills were the first thing that gave me the escape I needed at the time."

There was an awkward silence. I didn't understand why they wouldn't just drop it. I was beginning to regret the whole thing. I shouldn't have come to my first session with them. I had given them too much say so over my life. It wasn't about them, it was about me and my inner woes. I had to step away. I know it made me look weak. Maybe I was the weak one, but I had to step outside. I couldn't care less about the discussion that took place in my absence. I paced the yard, taking in the sweet scent of tomatoes and the spiciness of basil leaf. It was a pretty bright day. I enjoyed the heat radiating on my skin. If I was a christian, I guess it would have been my come to Jesus moment. But I was not a christian, the only religion I'd ever come close to adapting was buddhism, but I was not disciplined enough to maintain those practices. Anyways, I sat on the wooden swing in the front yard. My mind began to ramble. For the first time, I began to wonder who I was outside of chasing my dreams and apart from the accolades I had already established. I began to wonder who I was before I had been corrupted by the neglect and abandonment of my parents. That's when I started to realize that I was something much more important than the things I had attached myself to in order to feel important. I was alive, and my life was meant to be lived. No matter if people judged me, no matter if my choices went misunderstood. I was important, and I didn't have to explain myself if I felt it wasn't necessary. I appreciated my friends, but they didn't know me for me, they knew the me I had created to fit in their world and their ways of thinking. I realized that I had to define myself right then and there. I had to determine who Yaya was. I had to recognize my own voice. I had to become a mature adult, and let go of the past and all of the grudges, because if I didn't therapy would be a waste. If I continued to hold on to those awful burdens of the past I would continue to draw a wedge of distrust and betrayal in my friendships. I chose to be completely truthful with myself. I chose to forgive myself for all of the pain I had allowed myself to endure because I didn't think I was worthy.

I returned indoors, my friends were all eating, sort of quiet and observant of my mood. I sat between Chanel and Mercedes. They patted my thighs in a way to show their support.

"When I was twelve years old. I decided that I was going to be a lawyer. I read a book by Ernest J. Gaines called A Lesson Before Dying. That inspired me to be a powerful force in a monopoly that was set up to trap certain people for whatever reason. I decided that I was going to educate myself, and that I would be the important one. I would be so important that people would place their fate into my hands. I had made the decision that once I became a lawyer I would be important. I would win cases, and I would set myself free from the bottom pit. People would see me. And they would respect me because I was a lawyer, a damn good lawyer."

Everyone was quiet as if they were waiting on the point of my little speech. Maybe the way I had delivered the speech caused no response. But I did have a point. The point was that at twelve years old I had placed such a great expectation on myself, that I wouldn't feel complete until I met that goal. There I was, closer than I'd ever been but I felt more worthless than I've ever felt.

"Today, at twenty-six years old I decide that I am going to love myself just as I am. That may seem corny or even meaningless to you guys, but it is my newfound goal. It is the only thing I haven't tried. I don't need my parents to recognize me. I don't need another accolade to place me on a pedestal of importance. I am important, because I breathe. I am important because I love and I deserve to be loved, which first starts within me."

My friends hugged me. Chanel and Mercedes squeezed my hands into their palms. I think they had finally gotten the picture. I'm sure as they were my friends, my sisters, they shared the same goal. It was time that I healed, everything would work itself out if my health had become the highest priority.

"Yaya, you left out of here with so much fear and weakness in your eyes. What gave you the strength to walk back in here with so much poise and grace?"

"I'm no longer putting myself last. I don't have to run anymore, no one can make me feel less than. No one can block my healing."

"We got your back girl. Even if that means shutting our big mouths."

"Seriously, we need you pooh."

Dr. Moor, delved deeper into my upbringing. Although my friends were somewhat aware of my unfortunate childhood, they had been spared a lot of details. Dr. Moor needed that information in order for her to fully understand my world view and behavior towards life. I gave her the full rundown, and honestly we all just cried, everyone except the professional Dr. Moor that is. She handed us tissues and encouraged our tears. She asked me about my coming of age journey and my adolescent days. I explained to her that I was a loner. I didn't come out to my parents until I was twenty-one so most of those years from sixteen to twenty were lived in secrecy. I suffered through my first break up alone. I went to my prom alone, unhappy, and disconnected from my fellow classmates. Many of my embarrassing sexual experiences were because I had no one to talk to about sex. I didn't know how to make friends because I didn't feel free to be myself. I wasn't interested in boys, so they all thought I was stuck up and weird. I had very little in common with most of my female peers because they couldn't relate to having crushes on girls, let alone being heartbroken by one. I had found my solace in music and books. I read hundreds of books by the time I had reached eighteen. By the time I was twenty-one I was a walking thesaurus. I met Chanel and Angela through Mercedes. She was my roommate, but she was protective over me from the very start. She invited me to hang with her Ang and

Chanel whenever they made plans. She was the first to know and accept my sexuality. She didn't make any slick remarks about how she didn't agree with it or how she could never see herself with another girl, she simply told me that it was okay and that it was nothing to feel ashamed about. Chanel, however, did crack jokes. She said she couldn't picture me getting a bitch wet let alone pleasing a bitch with my tongue. Mercedes put her on blast, and told her that if she was bone straight like she claimed to be then that curiosity wouldn't have been in her head. Angela was cool with it, never had much to say about it either. They checked in on my love life here and there, but it was never a big interest of theirs since they knew I swung for the same team. Dr. Moor gave me an assignment. She told me to do something that puts me in the spotlight in a fun and easy going manner. These days all I wanted to do was be alone and closed off in my home, but she said there was no better time than now to get out of my comfort zone. I reluctantly agreed, feeling that I didn't have much of a choice.

"Yooo, what are we finna get into? I been needing a reason to get out." Chanel was bouncing with excitement. I already had something in mind. It was something I had never had the guts to do, but secretly wanted to do for so long.

"Karaoke!" I said.

They all laughed, knowing that it was so far from my comfort zone and my personality. But I was serious, it was a pipe dream that was finally going to come true.

"Wait, wait, Yaya. Girl are you serious?"

"Yes, I'm dead ass."

They laughed again, as Angela sped through traffic on the expressway to get us back on my side of town. We stopped by the mall in search of something sexy to wear for the night's outing. I settled for a sexy black backless halter top that I wore with denim jeans and wedge heels. Chanel wore a cutoff short body suit that barely covered her booty and six inch heels. Angela wore a sexy body suit, and Mercedes kept it classy with a pinstripe dress that emphasized her curves.

At the karaoke lounge we ordered nachos, wings, and drinks. I settled for a strawberry lemonade with no alcohol. I was aiming to be completely sober of any outside influences. My friends kept it light with daiquiris and martinis. The food was delicious. It was a decent crowd and the vibe was cool. I liked the variety of R&b and rap they played. The time came around to sign up for a shot on stage. I signed the sheet and patiently waited until it was my turn. I wasn't a good singer, but I had always loved this song by the Goo Goo Dolls called Iris. I was nervous as I took the stage. My friends cheered for me as the beat of the song played. I remembered how much the lyrics meant.

"I'll give up forever to touch you cause I know that you'd feel me somehow. You're the closest to heaven that I'll ever be and I don't wanna go home right now. All I can taste is this moment and all I can breathe is your life and sooner or later, it's over. I just don't wanna miss you tonight..."

To my surprise a lot of the crowd was familiar and sung along. Chanel recorded me and posted me to her Instagram. It didn't surprise me that I was made into a meme. My voice was so shaky. I was so overcome with emotion that it seemed at any moment I would cry as I sang. I look back on it and laugh. I was glad I'd taken Doc's advice. Chanel wanted to hit a nightclub since the night was still young. I was down. I had a burst of energy from following through with something that was totally out of my element and I felt good. We went to a popular club in downtown Memphis. It was already

248

packed to the walls, but there was still a line waiting to get in. Chanel made a phone call to whoever she knew and got us through the door without waiting. It was a mixed crowd, I could tell. LGBTQ was up and thriving right along with the straights. We shimmied our way straight to the dance floor. I held nothing back. I let my romp shake and let my hips swing. I was high off life and I didn't want to come down. My girls were giving it up for the men who had immediately approached them when we made it to the floor. I rejected the men who'd approached me, but I couldn't deny the soft hands that had caressed my waist and thrusted her goods into mine. I didn't face her at first. I just wanted to enjoy the feeling, but when the music slowed down a bit she turned me around to face her. It took everything inside of me to keep from laughing in her face. She was a weird looking girl. Her style was so corny. Too slim and short for her size of clothing. I smiled politely and walked away. I needed a cold drink.

"Water please." I yelled to the bartender.

" Water? Who are you trying to fool, love ?"

I turned around with slight disappointment. I thought I would be face to face with the baggy clothes weirdo. Instead I met the eyes of a fine stud woman. Inca had a sweet face, but her demeanor was confident with an edge about herself. Her energy was magnetic or maybe I was just thirsty in more ways than one. I leaned my body into hers and smiled.

"Why do you assume that I'm trying to fool someone?"

"Because these ungodly hours baby, everybody dabble in a little something to keep em lit."

"Who are you?"

"If dreams come true was a person."

"Cute, but what's your name?"

"Inca, yours?"

"Yaya."

"Cute."

"What do you want Inca?"

"I want Yaya, duh."

"A minute ago you didn't even know I existed, sweetheart."

"And my world was so blue without you."

"Girl stop it, your game is so cliche'. How many chicks fall for that line?"

Inca laughed, then studied me with seductive eyes. Though I was attracted I wanted to make her work a little. I could tell she was used to getting what she wanted.

"Nah, for real. I'm interested. I wanna get to know you. You know, take you out sometime."

"What if I'm taken?"

"Are you?"

"Would that change anything?"

Inca smirked. She knew I was giving her the run around by then. I liked teasing her for some reason, I don't know.

"Look Yaya, I don't know your situation. All I know is that a beautiful woman like yourself is something I don't see often. I may never see you again, but I'd be one weak ass nigga if I didn't shoot my shoot."

I sipped the last of my water. I had humbled the beast. I was very much impressed with myself. I took her hand in mine just to add the dramatic effect. "What would you do with me if I was all yours?"

"I'll love you through the darkness. I'll kiss your monsters away, and make love to your scars."

Inca's words left me speechless. No one had ever made me feel the way she did. I was beginning to believe in love at first sight. We didn't dance to G Eazy, ASAP Rocky, and Cardi B telling us it wasn't safe. We stood at the bar conversing about our journey that led us to the club. She was proud of me for seeking professional help, and she was inspired by my sisterhood with my girls. She was a software designer for Apple who had a lot of time on her hands and a decent enough income to go and do as she pleased. We'd just suggested to each other our favorite movies and books, when Chanel drunkenly interrupted us.

"Come Yaya, you can catch your booty call later, we need a designated driver and we is depending on you so come on."

Inca thought Chanel was the funniest thing ever. She walked us to the car, and I agreed to check in when I made it home safely. I kept my word and we fell asleep listening to each other's breathing over the phone.

***

I was deemed strong enough to have my home all to myself again. I awakened early in the morning before the sun had risen. Made myself a cup of ginger tea. Recited affirmations and stretched my body thoroughly before I headed out on my routine bike ride. I rode twenty-four miles, successfully. I didn't vomit or feel woozy after my bike rides anymore.

Aja sat on the wooden stomp on the pathway of our complex. She handed me a mason jar of cold water. It felt like ages since I've seen my young neighbor. Something was different about her. She seemed less enthusiastic than I'd remembered her. Then I remembered she was the one who'd found me overdosed in my apartment. The one who had saved my life. A sudden guilt came over me.

"How are you Aja? I missed you."

" I missed you too."

"So what's new? We have some catching up to do."

"Momma comes home next month. I got accepted into the STEM program and I have to complete my first science project."

"Wow that's all good news. I'm so happy for you Aja. Why don't you seem excited about all of this?"

"I am. I just wish you wouldn't have avoided me for so long then I would have been told you this."

"I wasn't avoiding you Aja. I was sick, but I'm much better now. I'm getting the help I need."

Aja shook her head, then dropped it. Sadness consumed her. "You could have died. If you would've died then I would be alone. You're my bestest friend Yaya."

I hugged her compassionately. "I'm sorry for scaring you. I never meant for you to see me like that."

"I always keep your scary secrets. Remember that night you thought people were chasing you? Or that night you fell asleep half naked on your porch? I saw a lot of stuff and I always worry about you. Every Night I pray that you make it home safe, and I pray that you wake with good health too."

I didn't know I meant so much to Aja. I guess I never thought about the role I played in her life, maybe I didn't take it seriously. But I could see the trauma I had caused her. I felt obligated to make things right between us. I could never repay her for saving my life, even if I didn't want to be saved. I was much stronger now. I saw reality more clearly. My choices were healthier.

"I want to apologize but I know saying sorry isn't good enough. It won't take away the pain I caused you and it won't make you forget all those times I made you afraid. So I won't say sorry. But I do want you to get the chance to know me, the better version of me that is. Let's start over. Okay?"

"I don't think so Yaya. You want to act like nothing ever happened, but I can't pretend. I'm not a little kid. I know things. I'm smart, and I know you overdosed on drugs. I just don't know why. Why would you do that?"

"Aja, the answer is more complicated than I think you're ready to understand. But I just felt so much pain. I was hurting, sweetheart. And I wanted a release."

"I hate that. Don't tell me I'm too young to understand. My momma was a dope head. Kids my age are dope heads. I see and hear a lot of things. I know stuff."

" I don't take you for a fool at all, Aja. I didn't mean to offend you. What I meant to say is that it's not easy to explain. But maybe on one of our bike rides we could talk everything through."

"What? I don't have a bike, Yaya."

"Then we have to get you one because I need a riding buddy."

"What! Are you for real?"

"Yes, I'll get you the new bike, everything's on me. It's not much but it's a start."

Aja hugged me with so much gratitude and love. I couldn't help but kiss her precious cheeks. She was like a sister and a daughter all in one. We made a trip to Walmart. Aja was so excited to be in my company. She was a good girl and it did something for my self worth to be able to make her happy. She picked out a sky blue 10 speed Giant. It cost me nearly two hundred dollars but the tears of joy Aja shed as she thanked me were priceless. Turns out Aja had thought of a complicated but extremely intriguing hypothesis for her science project.

"Flowers are like us. They are more human than actual humans. They can breathe. They listen. They need water and natural lighting just like us in order to grow and survive. They need oxygen like we do too."

"That's great Aja, there are plenty of people who don't see any importance in nature. It's so easy to take its beauty for granted."

"See that's the thing. That's why with my experiment I want to plant flowers somewhere that they won't be taken for granted. People will have to acknowledge them."

I laughed. Aja acted as if she had to give me some kind of pitch before she introduced her idea for the project. It was adorable to see her so passionate about something though.

"Where will you sow them?"

"In the concrete."

So, there you have it. We searched the gardening section of Walmart for Cosmos and Snapdragon seeds. Hours later we were planting and watering the seeds through the crests of the concrete, on the sidewalk of our apartment complex. It was a fulfilling experience. We broke a healthy sweat, enjoyed Ms. Mabel's homemade peach tea as she snapped pictures of us. I had dinner at their home. Chicken dumplings, broccoli, and buttered rice. I made a silent vow to remain consistent in Aja' life no matter what.

***

Inca and I were getting serious, and she'd invited me to go on a vacation out of the country with her. I trusted Inca and didn't doubt her intentions, but I had to be an adult on the matter. I invited the girls over to my place for dinner, so they could formally meet Inca, my new lover.

I had a taste for Mexican food, so I cooked enchiladas and tacos. We ate in my living room, as we gave Jhene Aiko's new album a listen.

"So, Inca do you take all of your women out of the country with you after one month of dating or is our little Yaya just that special?" Angela asked, sipping her third glass of Chardonnay.

"No, I don't take every woman I date out of the country with me. But I figured my woman who I made it official with would be interested in this trip based on conversations we've had and I want to do something special for my lady." Inca replied, the way she spoke of me sent chills down my spine.

"What the fuck kind of name is Inca, no offense?" Chanel blurted.

"It's my heritage. My people descended from Peru. It has two meanings, I guess, one is the South American hummingbird and the other means royal from the Incan empire." Inca responded to Chanel's ignorant question with such patience.

"That's real cool. So that's why you're taking my friend to Peru. It's starting to make sense now." Chanel replied.

I knew they were giving Inca a hard time for my sake, but she was so easy to love. Everything about her was so genuine and loveable. She had almond shaped eyes, full chocolate lips, waves that could make a dolphin sea sick. She smelled like apple cinnamon. Her attire was always neat and crisp. What wasn't there to like? Even though my friends weren't lesbian, they couldn't deny Inca's attractiveness. They were doing their best to protect me, though. It had been a while since I've dated someone, so me being in a relationship was new to them. However, they had better adjust quickly.

" How long is this trip gonna be?" Mercedes quizzed.

"Two weeks." I replied.

"Will this affect your school work?" Mercedes asked.

"No, I got this Mercedes." I said. She could be such a mom at times.

Chanel glanced between Inca and me, then pursed her lips and rolled her eyes.

"Um, well shit you grown, if you like it I love it."

"Thanks Chanel."

"Ooh honey no, you're not off the hook just yet. How will we keep in touch with you while you're a million miles away for these two weeks?"

"You won't be. We are giving up our phones. We'll be in a rainforest where there is little to no technology."

"What the fuck Yaya? You know we worry about you and have good reason to do so. So why are you cool with being somewhere we can't reach you?"

"I'm going to be fine Mercedes. It's no reason to worry about me."

Inca pulled out her phone, "This is a number you could reach Yaya when you get a lil weary of her whereabouts. It's my great granny's house phone. The only phone there is in the small village."

I breathed a sigh of relief. Mercedes acted so worried she almost made me second guess my trip.

"Aww see, she's looking out for us. That's important Inca because we're a package deal sweetie." Angela said.

Inca nodded, handing Mercedes her phone so she could add the contact. "Of course I respect the sisterhood. No doubt." Inca said. I could tell she'd made a good impression on my girls.

***

Truthfully, real life could be stranger than fiction sometimes. Two month ago I was a suicidal addict suffering from undiagnosed bipolar disorder. Fast forward to today I'm on a plane ride with my new found love who feels more like my soulmate. We share a bag of her favorite sweet potato chips and watch How To Get Away With Murder on her iPad. It feels heavenly to be close to her. Seven hours later we were greeted by her uncle and aunt in the airport.

"Inca, le damos la bienvenida a sobrina, ha pasado tanto tiempo." Inca's uncle hugged her dearly and kissed her cheek.

"Gracias senor."

Her aunt squeezed her gently and smiled. "How are you?"She asked.

"I'm well Senorita. I'm very well." Inca said.

"You must be her love, Yaya?" Her uncle asked.

"Yes sir, that's me." I went for a handshake and got a tender-loving hug instead. I had expected Inca's family to have a light complexion with soft fair hair, instead they had kinky hair and Black American features. I felt ignorant to believe Black people only existed in certain parts of the world.

It took us thirty minutes to make it to their village. Once we got there we were greeted by thirteen more of her relatives. Most of them were elders, only a few were children and adolescents. Everyone was peculiarly polite and respectful. Inca's personality began to make more and more sense to me. Inca's great grandmother had prepared a plentiful homestyle peruvian meal for our welcome. My favorite dishes were Papa a la huancaina and the Jalea. I washed it down with Maca nectar, and was more than satisfied with the quality of Peruvian food. After dinner, we sat in the living room looking through family photo albums. Apparently, consistent yearly trips to Peru had been a major part of Inca's upbringing. Not even two hours into our stay, Inca's great grandmother's home phone rang.

"Oh wow, that old thing never rings. Must be important." Inca's uncle said. Inca gave me a knowing look then smirked.

"Yaya, it's for you." Inca's uncle said with a confused grin.

I playfully shoved Inca, because I realized she was teasing me, and rolled my eyes as I pressed the phone to my ear. "Hi moommm." I said sarcastically into the phone."

"Girl whatever, I'm calling to check up on you since you don't have the decency to let anybody know you made it across the world safely." Mercedes replied on the other end.

"I'm sorry girl, all of this is new to me. I wasn't thinking." I said.

"Tell me something I don't know. How is your trip so far? Are you settling in nicely?" She asked.

"They are great people. I'm enjoying myself a whole lot."

"Good, that's good. Give Inca my gratitude. And check in every once in a while or else I'll be on your ass."

"Okay, Mercedes. I love you girl."

"I love you more, bye."

Inca stared at me from across the room with a lustful look that I'd grown all to familiar with. I shifted in my stance nervously and glanced around at her family. They weren't paying us any mind. Inca walked out of the door and I followed behind moments later. There was a pathway that led to the forest. The sun was setting, foreign birds soared low enough to clip my messy bun. Inca was quiet, something about her mysterious aura intrigued me. I was curious about the direction we were heading, but I didn't question her. I just took her hand in mine. She gripped my hand and pressed it against her lips. I stiffened with fear when I felt a rough sensation upon my shoulder. Inca looked over at me and smiled beautifully, so beautiful that it calmed me.

"Marvellous spat, he's a messenger." Inca said. It was the tiniest, prettiest little bird I'd never seen. Grey, purple and blue, his beak was tiny and thin, but his tail was the most gorgeous thing about him, two long racquet-shaped outer feathers that crossed each other with violet-blue discs on the ends. Also known as spatules, hence his name. He walked the rest of the path with us. We stopped by the shore of a deep blue rainfall.

"Everything about this place amazes me. I'm in awe at every little detail." I said. The Marvellous Spat went humming on its way as Inca softly sucked my lips into hers. She grabbed my waist as I hugged her neck. She untied my halter top and let my breasts bounce in the evening breeze.

I wanted to eat her alive. She was so sweet and good to me. She kissed me all over until my legs got weak and I shook to the ground. She fingered me through my panties. She was so dominant. I could only surrender. Inca was one track minded when it came to pleasing me, my every wish was her command. I orgasmed countless times near that waterfall. I was so relaxed, so in tune with the nature around me. Wrapped in my lover's arms, I couldn't stop the freefall of tears from my eyes.

"I don't wanna become addicted to you." I said,

"What do you mean baby?" Inca asked, concerned.

"I don't wanna get over one habit just to adapt another one. I'm happy to have you but I think this is a vulnerable time for me right now. I might become too dependent on you."

"Yaya, don't overthink this. You're strong with or without me. You made the decision to heal way before I came into your life. Don't blur the lines."

"I'm not. I don't mean to. This just feels too good to be true and when the good runs out I don't wanna relapse because of the pain."

" I won't hurt you. Even if I make a mistake or disappoint you it's up to you to find your own strength. You have to learn to detach from shit that overly consumes you."

"But how?"

"You gotta face your demons. I mean really face the darkest shit within yourself without running or judging it."

"I can't do that."

"You can and we in the perfect place to guide you through that."

"What do you mean?"

"My aunt and uncle curate Ayahuasca trips, they last up to seven days. Some people have their breakthrough in three days, it all depends on the depth of your demons and trauma."

"What are Ayahuasca trips?"

"It is a plant that grows right here in South America. My aunt and uncle allow people into our village and guide them as they use the plant as a psychedelic medicine. It takes people through all types of wild trips in their mind. At every phase everyone experiences different things, but everyone physically releases the sickness that's been haunting them."

"How convenient. Did you plan this Inca? Cause you could have just told me."

"What? Nah. It's just a suggestion, you can easily say no and you won't hear nothing else about it."

I thought through it for about five minutes before I made my mind up. I didn't believe in coincidences, I also knew Inca wasn't coercing me into something

I wasn't comfortable with. It was my realization of the gift of miracles. I chose healing so the universe aligned me with resources and a tribe of people that would sincerely guide me through.

I sat on the patio of the cabin house Inca's aunt and uncle owned. They were boiling the Ayahuasca plant in order to preserve it's fluid for me to consume like a beverage. The first phase was the easiest compared to the other three phases, but it was somehow extremely difficult for me. My father was a successful dentist. He owned three offices in the greater Memphis area. My mother was a postal worker. Their incomes afforded me admittance into one of the top private schools in Memphis. I remember being the only black child in attendance for several years. One day in history class the topic of slavery came up. My peers and my teacher spoke of slavery like it was some kind of free labor, instead of the horriffic genocide and famicide it inflicted upon black people. Even as a young child I knew these things. I did a lot of reading by the time I was thirteen years old, I'd studied Carter G. Woodson, Angela Davis, and James Baldwin. They were my father's favorite authors and mainly all I had to choose from our at home library. I understood that there were undermining tactics of systematic suppression and the passive tactics that were orchestrated to maintain stagnancy and disorder among Black Americans. I was thirteen. An eighth grader at her wits end with the brutal gestures and methods of my peers and my authority figures, of which they used to silence and undermine my perspectives and my intelligence. I became enraged, so enraged that I threw a book at my teacher's head. The class was so distraught and appalled that they gasped in unison and watched me like they had seen the devil in the flesh. The teacher yelled at me to go to the office. "Who do you think you are?" She shouted. I knew deep down, though she hadn't said it aloud, I knew that was her way of calling me a nigger. Picture me sitting angrily on a swing with my cornrowed head bowed, as my father and mother spoke with the principal and assistant principal about my fate at the school. Every other second I would peep up from the short distance of the playground, and across the parking lot I could see them inside the principal's office through the open blinds. Those people, my parents, never understood. They didn't take my insubordinate actions as a cry for help. I wanted to free myself from that mental suppression. I wanted to be a part of my culture. I needed to feel the life and the breath of children with skin and hair like mine, but since they thought our school's were not good enough, since they thought their money made them more entitled, they fought for me to remain at the all white private because it was considered the best of the best. I sat in the backseat of my father's Expedition as he and my mother bragged and boasted about their accomplishment. There I was in my black suit jacket with gold and green embroidery and my dark green and black plaid skirt, crying. Literally crying as they spoke. "Gladly we've positioned ourselves to be the distinguished ones. That when we talk they listen. Money is a weapon they can't defeat, even when they so badly want to." My father said. Which proved it was about their egos, it had zero to do with my well being and my dreams. I was to remain at a school I hated to prove a point to black high society. That's the beginning of my identity crisis, that's when my feelings of unworthiness and emptiness became solidified. The shame, regret, and sorrow came pouring out of me in the form of diarrhea. I sharted for two hours straight. I thought I would die. I was severely dehydrated. All I could do was drink and sleep the entire next day. Inca was told to remain away from me during the duration of my trips, in order to maintain an essential stability throughout the entire process. The first phase was many journeys and revisiting of my earlier life as a child and adolescent. The second phase was indescribable. I truly believe I experienced death it's complete form. I saw faces and places that were so terrifying that I stopped breathing. I would awake from these trips woozy and discombobulated. I was so disoriented that I didn't know where I was and how I'd got there. I vomited ferociously. I cursed out Inca's aunt and uncle. I was violent and angry for reasons I could not explain. This phase was the longest. I had trouble getting through to the third phase. It was so scary that I cried for my mother and father, but it infuriated me more to know that they would never come to my rescue. It took eight total days to fully recover and overcome the phases of every trip. The third phase was so beautifully terrifying that I would hold onto that memory and that feeling for the rest of my days. For I can say that I know heaven and God is real.

Inca's family allowed me to rest and to spend most of my time after the Ayahuasca trip in solitude. Her great grandmother gifted me with a book of ancient Incan parables and a journal. They made sure I ate nourishing food that would rejuvenate my mind and body healthily.

Inca and I spent our last two days in Peru sitting in her great granny's company. The woman was very wise. I explained to her that I was two steps away from being a qualified lawyer. She then explained to me the history of healers. How many healers are first the broken people. Healers are to experience suffering that most people would succumb to, but the Most High is always covering them. She said my blackness causes me to pursue the illusion of excellence, so that I could be a savior to those who aren't equipped to reach the same high achievements. She called this the Black Messiah Syndrome. Inca's great grandmother told us that many young Black American women suffered from the Black Messiah Syndrome due to the lack of love and support of black femininity. Since Black women weren't allowed to be soft and sensitive they took on the role of saviors and high achieving leaders which robbed them of their God given feminine nature.

"Many people shun Christ because he was odd. He took no credit for his alchemy. He glorified a higher power in a hedonistic era. He gave God the glory and people envied him. He was a rebel and an outcast, but he led others to their salvation and healing. He produced healers and leaders not followers. He didn't discriminate as the world would expect, all was worthy of healing. All except those who denied it. You do not have to heal others, because when you heal yourself you inspire others to do the same. Focus solely on yourself. Love only yourself, then you will naturally love others." She said.

Inca's family sent us off with our hearts and bellies full. I wanted to stay in Peru, but I knew I had to return home. The flight back seemed shorter. Maybe because we slept the whole way through.

Mercedes and Angela met us at the airport. Mercedes' attitude was a little stank, but I hugged her and kissed her cheek. I needed her to feel my love. I had to show her that I wasn't the same broken girl that had left two weeks ago. Angela and I hugged each other. She happily welcomed us back, and acknowledged my newly awakened glow. Chanel was out of town on a business venture, but I spoke with her on the phone on the ride back to my place. She was happy for me but encouraged me to stick with therapy. I told her I would.

We pulled into the parking lot of my apartment complex. I saw Aja on the sidewalk, watering the growing Cosmos and Snapdragons. I was in disbelief that the flowers were blooming less than a month from sowing them. Aja's hypothesis was legit. There were flowers in the concrete of our complex, no one could ignore their beauty. Aja would make sure of it.

***

Hannah Abdullah Muhammad was designated at Tennessee's State Prison for women. She'd been on a hunger strike for three months and had been out of solitary confinement for ten days up and until our visit. She was so thin, but nothing about her looked fragile or sickly. She took both of my hands into hers and tilted her head towards me.

"As-Salaam-Alaikum." She greeted me. Her tone was stern and proud.

"Wa-Alaikum-Salaam" I replied respectfully.

We sat down simultaneously, never breaking eye contact. Her twelve neat braids hung like ropes from her moisturized scalp. I didn't see a victim. I didn't see a criminal. Yes, she was an artist, but she exuded an intellect that could have easily placed her in a position of a judge or a rightful president. She could have easily been in my suit and I could have been her state property uniform.

"I knew this day would come." Muhammad said. And I breathed a sigh of relief.

Muhammad was truly a diamond in the rough. There was no denying her powerful and godly presence. I knew then that I was not her savior, but I was a warrior and comrade standing on the frontline of a war we were prepared to win. Just as she had fasted, and seemingly starved herself in order to manifest a dream she was destined to make true, so had I faced my demons and fasted them away. She didn't see the drug addict or the victim mentality I once carried inside, instead she saw me as a strong figure she could trust.

A GHETTO SCI-FI

By

Damita Taylor

Paranoia plays a game of tug-a-war with her mind. Afflicted by chaos. Haunted by shrills of unknown beings. They make plans to dictate her psyche and overthrow her true memory. All she can do is lie still with hopes that they'll cease eventually, as usual. Her heart's cry is muffled, heavy and hollow. Lights of green, red, and the sharpest white pierce her vision. It is midnight on a Saturday. Nyeema is cradled beneath her comforter in the blackness of her bedroom. Silent salty tears smudge her face. She wants to drown out the wicked noises, but she is rendered helpless. The line between nightmares and reality are blurred. The paranoia within instigates senseless suspicions. Laughter and conversation coming from unfamiliar people, she thinks invaded the house, seeps under the doorsill of her bedroom.

"Hellooo. Is anybody there?!! Hehe hee!" The voice of an obnoxious evil sounding woman howls. The voices are jumbled and clash as they speak to her all at once. Some of it is chattering like being in a crowded restaurant. Others are so loud and distinct she thinks she may lose her hearing and that her cranium will explode. *"Destroy! Destroy! Nothing is worthy. It is all an illusion!"* A wicked voice shrills and rattles her skull.

Echoes. False cries. Intrusion. Deceptive emotions screwing with her mental peace and good judgement. When she doesn't believe they rant, rave, and curse her until she does. Their threats are loaded with pain and unfair warning. Growing more frantic, Nyeema starts to yelp and groan. Her pleas are slurred. Her breathing flow is desperate and faint. Her nerves are in an uproar. Death threats from unseen hell raisers wreak havoc upon her. Like being trapped on a turbulent charged rollercoaster from hell. She is woozy, wheezing, and nauseated. She tries to scream but her cries are smothered by an invisible muzzle.

The tickle of death numbs her feet. The bloodiest brightest red light electrocutes her entire body, sending her into a state of epileptic shock. A vision of a girl with a dismembered face and gashes through her throat consumes her. A greenish-black serpent emerges out of the thick belly of a black mudded swamp. Nyeema squirms. Her tongue is heavy and dry. Panicking. Her heart slams against her breast cage. She wants to plead one last cry for help, but it is too late.

The serpent flashes its yellowish spiked fangs and flicks its red double wedged tongue. The reptilian swallows her whole. Nyeema' body quakes, bearing the commotion of a spacecraft looming from earth's edge. The sound of rambunctious metal screeching then clashing into a collision of ginormous buildings provokes an impenetrable sensation within her. Freezing cold water pouring into boiling hot water perplexes her senses. Bleeding ears. The fist of twelve gorillas pounds at her skull. An agony too gruesome and peculiar to scribe. It is surreal, extremely. Engulfed in a tornado of a bottomless ocean she falls at full-fledged speed. A cosmic blue projection of herself levitates in the capsule of a red and yellow neon light wave. A fuzzy static sound charges into her temples, causing a light to glow where her heart should be.

The celestial planet of mythic creations, Terra Supra Neomenia, looms from a total eclipse.

Her burgundy and gold vapory sky evokes a kaleidoscopic horizon. Her sun gleams above a peach, violet, and turquoise ocean. Licorice trees bend, stretch, and intertwine like ballerinas. Pathways of tanzanite stone dazzle the land. Two-toned, burgundy-blue, flying saucers roam low and high. Lapis Lazuli pyramid huts align the landscape of the celestial plane.

    Nagaa Ra and Sa Nut, the father and mother of Terra Supra Neomenia, are seated scorpion style with the slender legs hidden under their silver metallic hooded robes. They watch Nyeema through a virtual screen on an orbiting monitor. Nagaa Ra, speaks a dialect of three vowels, "o", "u", and "e", using his throat to emphasize their meaning. Sa Nut responds to him in the same dialect. Nut whistles, and a chalk substance powder the lair.

Nyeema emerges from the openness that forms from the powder covered with a clear slime. She rests inside a hologram incubator that floats in the air. She is experiencing the frequency of sound and light on a supernatural level, though her avatar form lay in the presence of Nagaa Ra and Sa Nut. Her conscience vibrates in an ether that is galaxies away.

An array of vibrant colors glow within the transparency of her avatar, creating a vast spectrum of geometrical shapes and patterns. Nagaa Ra and Sa Nut are two bluish-black creatures with leather smooth skin. They wear masks of beaks and jewels rotating purple and silver beads pierced into their pineal glands. Their cerulean eyes pulsate as they watch Nyeema ' avatar multiply into five different auras fields, bronze, lime, shamrock, orange, and purple. Nagaa Ra and Sa Nut stand up simultaneously. Hovering over Nyeema like enamored new parents in awe of their newborn child, they examine her closer. Nut blows a powder substance into Nyeema ' avatar, and sways her hands over her body like she is performing magic.

Nyeema 'transforms back into her natural flesh. Her eyes shoot open. She lay naked, there in a serene state. Nagaa Ra raises the shield of the incubator and lifts Nyeema into his winged arms. She detects his powerful strength, but feels as if she's being carried by a feather. Nyeema is overwhelmed by uncertainty, but she is unable to put any questions into word form, instead she blinks helplessly. They glide into a lair of ultra-beaming light. There is a pool of steamy water in the center of the luminous room. Nagaa places Nyeema into the pool, which to her surprise is freezing cold and has great depth.

"Brace yourself." Nut says in a hypnotic tone.

Instantly, Nyeema submerges deep into its abyss at boundless full-fledged speed. There are no stops. Everything is out of her control. Howling sinister laughter erupts, taunting her. Spiked thorns pierce and aggravate her. The all too familiar chaotic voices arise and harass her, as she spirals lower and lower.
"Fire!" An unknown being shrills and bleeds her ears.

Nyeema is plunged into the wrath of scorching lava. She yearns to scream for dear life but is unable to make a sound. Haphazardly a collage of horrendous beasts charge at her. A six-legged deformed demon laughs goofily as he dances around her, igniting her with immense nausea. Another terrifying webbed head reptilian type creature growls a deadly threat of venom her way. Wicked cackles and whispers of unseen affliction haunts her. She begins reciting psalms 23 silently to herself. Aunt Kemet taught her there's psalm for every circumstance, and their weight is awesomely powerful. A meteoric boom explodes, sending her floating into a sea of darkness and an ethereal silence.

"Breathe, baby." The voice Nyeema hears may as well be a voice from an angle. It silences everything.

Nyeema becomes calm. There is no combustion of howls and blabbering. She lay in her momma's lap under a soft blue sunny sky. The waves of the ocean kisses the shore. The smell of salt and clean spring air clears her nostrils. Her momma's loving hand may as well be the graze of her favorite blanket. Nyeema looks up to Asia. Her momma feels real, warm, strong. Her momma's smile is a quiet counsel, saying that she is safe now. She is always safe. Nyeema wants to say so much, but it has been so long. Ten long bitter years, and nothing that is meaning has to be said. Because they know. The love they share is boundless, unconditional, unbreakable. Nyeema does not want to ruin the moment. Unbeknownst to Nyeema, Asia is her guardian angel. One call, one prayer, one cry away. Asia rocks Nyeema as if to say you are still momma's baby. Together they sun gaze and listen to the music of nature. Heaven must be like this. Worries disappearing in the arms of a loving mother. Nyeema grips her momma's hand and rubs her teary cheek on her lap. But swift like the breeze that chills her spine, it comes to an end her momma crumbles and becomes sand. Nyeema panics, gripping the sand that vanishes, the sea is gone, leaving her in midair of nowhere.

Sobbing and gasping Nyeema opens her eyes. Lying in her bed flustered and dismayed. She fights to digest all that she's experienced in such a short moment. The voices are quieted. Her heart races. She feels alien to her environment. Her senses are enhanced. David Ruffin "I Miss You" plays on the living room stereo. The words sing to her soul. For a long time she's missed her momma.

Asia was a fierce woman, playful and free spirited, but serious about her role as a woman and mother. Nyeema has had selective memory when it came to Asia's death. As of now everything is open. Her heart, mind, emotions of good, old, and sad are pouring out of her like the sweat that drips from her temples onto her cheeks.

Early on, at age six to be exact, Nyeema felt that it was selfish to miss her momma. That her sadness would somehow make her momma sad. Knowing that it was not her momma's fault that she was not here with her. Like a bird in an impassioned whirl of wind, Asia's spirit flew from her body and Nyeema was her witness. Unable to truly compartmentalize the dread of loneliness that accompanied her ever since her momma passed away Nyeema made herself feel guilty and convinced herself that it did not matter. The pain that weighed against her was too great to bear. But tonight as David Ruffin sings from a place that only those in great pain can feel, Nyeema lets those warm tears flow. Yearning for what was stolen. She was there the day her daddy barricaded himself and her momma inside her momma's bedroom. Asia begged him to calm down for their daughter. She begged him to stop beating her. The punches were gruesome and terrorizing. The seven gunshots were deafening and paralyzing. Nyeema was there. Locked away in her bedroom, tucked beneath a pile of sheets in her closet. Her daddy fled the scene how thieves and destroyers do. Nyeema remembered that he didn't even shut the door to the house, and her momma's blood was soaking into the carpet fast. Asia was still breathing, struggling, dying, still breathing. She coughed thick chunks of dark blood that looked purple. Nyeema can taste the salty warm smell as she lay in bed, unable to escape what she has so long avoided. Asia kept saying sorry. Nyeema was afraid and shocked, she did not shed a tear. The paramedics and police arrived too late. Her momma had flown away, somewhere beyond the walls of their home and above the bounds of the earth. Nyeema felt like dying. She wanted to go to the place that her momma so peacefully accepted. After begging for her life and apologizing until her last breath to her one and only child. The paramedics had to peel Nyeema ' hands from her momma's face. Nyeema had been holding her, hoping that it was all a bad dream. But it was real, and she has regretted the day ever since. She wished that she could tell her momma that she needn't be sorry. But as a girl on the tip of womanhood she understands her momma's meaning. She knew that life would be incomplete for a motherless and fatherless daughter. Nyeema daddy was murdered while on the run from the cops less than a year later. Asia was sorry for her choice of man she'd so mistakenly produced a child with. Sorry for being too weak to be done when he first abused her. She knew it was too late and she was sorry about that.

As Nyeema sulks in bed, she digests the epiphany that greets her. Because she kept herself from missing and mourning the loss of her momma, she missed her chance to celebrate her momma and have those sweet angelic connections, which were gifted to those that are loved and also missed by those on the other side.

Thin walls do talk. Nyeema hears Kemet on the phone arguing with Rome who is her children's daddy and her high school sweetheart turned sour. She found out he was cheating on her and had produced a side baby with the other woman. Maybe Kemet is confused on who left who because every so often she calls him and nags him for forgetting where home's at.

"Boy bye, ain't nobody trippin off you. Shit if anything you the one that got shit twisted. What? Nigga please. Yea they are good. They are good because I make sure they are good. Nigga fuck you." The music volume rises to the roof. Nyeema is unnerved. She needs something to quench her thirst, but hates that she has to pass by her aunty in the living to get to the kitchen. Yet, and still, against her better judgement and defeated by a dry mouth, Nyeema rises from bed to get a cold beverage. As soon as Nyeema turns the hallway corner and steps

swiftly into the living room, Kemet stops her in her tracks.

"Niecy pooh, it's three in the morning, what are you doing up so late? These demon hours, you that girl?" Kemet's southern drawl is more slowed and relaxed from the weed and half pint of cognac she indulges as she listens to her oldies. Dressed in her work scrubs from her late night shift as a nursing assistant at The Med. Her playlist shuffles to David Ruffin 'Statue of a Fool'. Although Kemet's big dimpled smile is challenging, lighting up the low lit room, Nyeema can tell her aunty is tired, her big bright brown eyes are low and red. The effect of the weed and liquor.
In a hoarse tone Nyeema replies, "I'm just getting some juice. I'm thirsty."

"Girl juice is just going to make you thirstier. Drink some water. And why are you up late and thirsty? What's going on?" Kemet presses her.

Nyeema takes heed to her aunt's suggestion and grabs the cold pitch of purified water and pours herself two glasses. She downs them both in one gulp, then pours herself a glass of lemonade. Her thirst is quenched, but the juice is for mere pleasure. "Goodnight aunty." Nyeema says.

Kemet studies her niece. Nyeema wears a pink cami top with shorts to match. She's transformed from a beautiful little girl to an evenly gorgeous young woman right before Kemet's eyes. Nyeema is filling out well, and that scares Kemet.

"Come here, niece." Kemet says, patting the couch pillow next to her. Nyeema is hesitant, unsure.

"Bring your butt here, girl." Kemet says putting pep in Nyeema ' step. Nyeema places her cup on the coffee table, clearly she is uneasy. Kemet is humored, she laughs.

"Damn girl. I am your aunty not the damn feds, relax."

For some reason the word relax makes the hairs on Nyeema ' neck stand up and she becomes shame-faced. Kemet watches Nyeema , observing her tense posture. Nyeema is a spitting image of her momma, Kemet's older sister. Kemet' heart swells just thinking of her sister. They were close to say the least. Nyeema inches toward her lemonade.

"You ain't fucking yet is you?" Kemet asks. Nyeema chokes. The lemonade travels down the wrong pipe and she coughs something violent. Kemet is a straight shooter, not one for small talk. She never seems to fall short at throwing Nyeema off guard. Nyeema stares at her aunty, flabbergasted. Kemet shrugs.

"I just asked a question." She replies.

Nyeema answers, still taken aback, "Aunty, I'm sixteen."
Kemet ducks down laughing, "Girl, I was fifteen when I started fucking. I know girls nowadays starting earlier than that."
Nyeema shrugs and shakes her head. "Well I'm not other girls, Aunty."

Kemet presses her lips to her blunt, nodding her head, satisfied with Nyeema's answer.

"So what are you doing, saving it for marriage, waiting on somebody special?" Kemet eases on her question.

Nyeema ponders. Eye to eye with her aunty, she replies, "I never thought about it, that's all. I mean people my age talk about doing it and how it's supposed to feel. But I haven't actually thought about doing it, not yet."

Kemet nods. "Not yet. Good. You know you are beautiful right? And you are valued, lil heffa you."

Nyeema nods.

"Good. When girls don't know they beautiful they get to looking for a nigga to validate that for'em. I'm not having that. I know it's always a nigga in the street ready to play head games with your child. I ain't having it."

Nyeema rolled her eyes, annoyed at the thought. She knows the type her aunty speaks of. Plenty of over age men approach her with sexual gestures and weak compliments when she walks to the park, the corner store, or waits on the bus line to go get art supplies and visit art exhibits. Which reminds her to ask her aunty' permission for an Uber account, later when she's sober.

"Don't trip, aunty. You don't have to worry. I 'm not one of those stupid girls with rose colored glasses. It doesn't excite me just because some dude says I'm cute." Nyeema proclaims.

Kemet smiles proudly and chuckles to herself. "I know that's right, niece. I did a good job with you girl. Your momma would be proud of me. You better than us when we were your age and that's all a momma can ask for." Kemet's voice quakes and she is teary eyed. "Just know I'm here when you are ready to have that talk. Sex apart of nature it ain't nothing to be ashamed about. You hear me?" Kemet says.

Nyeema smiles. "Yes ma'am." She replies.

"Give aunty some love, little girl." And like a soundtrack to a photo album slideshow Closer than Close by Atlantic Starr plays as they embrace lovingly. A real hug, what they both needed in the first place.

***

Nyeema is having a harsher day. Mentally she is more agitated than usual and hypersensitive. Nyeema vacuums the inner cushions of the couches. Shaka is in an ordinary playful mood. Day to day, his childish antics include getting on somebody's nerves, especially Nyeema. Except today, Nyeema is fighting a losing battle with her mind. The voices in her head are daring her to do homicidal, detrimental exploits. Between Shaka's highly irritating singing along to the music that blasts from Jahrome' bedroom stereo, and the enraged voices inside her unquiet mind, Nyeema is going insane. She is losing balance and grip of her own thoughts. The screws of her psyche are loosened. Shaka jumps up and down from each couch as Nyeema cleans and fluffs the pillows. He spins the wet rag, he's half cleaned the kitchen counters with, above his head.

"Something wicked this way comes. Something wicked. This way comes." He chats the old school Tupac lyrics into lyrics face waving the wet rag at her. So oblivious to her level of rage. Nyeema feels as though her cerebrum is being stung by thousands of swarming bees. His voice adds fuel to the gruesome fire that condemns her. Nyeema's eyes are crazy and deranged. She is in a trance, an altered state of mind. Possessed by entities more powerful than she. Once, and one time only she yells through the excruciating pain, "Cut it out, Shaka!"

Shaka bounces down on the short couch with a silly paused expression. He acts like he is scared and heeding to her demand. His hands are up in surrender as she passes him by to go into the kitchen.

Nyeema faces the kitchen window above the sink, spaced out. Shaka runs in and slaps her exposed arms with the wet rag. "Sike." Shaka's tiny voice sings as he dances and hops around, acting like a monkey. "Wicked, wicked, wicked." He sings Future' lyrics. Remixing the two songs together. Nyeema grabs a steak knife from the cutlery and chases Shaka through the house. She sees red, dying from the worst possible migraine. She catches

Shaka by the collar, and in a swift motion he twists from her grip and dashes for Jahrome' room.

Jahrome sits on his floor painting a pair of white and red retro 6 Jordan's glittery silver and midnight blue. Shaka hauls in screaming at the top of his lungs, "Help. She trying to kill me." Nyeema waltzes in like a mad serial killer with the pointed knife, aiming straight for Shaka. Making a quick evaluation, Jahrome hops on his feet and shields Shaka. "Yo E, chill. You have to put that knife down. My momma will kill me if you kill bruh." Jahrome says calmly. To Nyeema his voice is faint and distant like talking under water. Nyeema zones in on Shaka like a shark that smells blood.

"Noooo, pleaseee." Shaka whines. Taking refuge behind his brother's back. Jahrome eases backward. It is becoming too clear to him that his cousin is not fully there. Nyeema is the calm one, even now as she aims a knife ready to murder his little brother she is calm somehow.

"E, cuzzo. Please. Put the knife away. He playful as fuck but this ain't that serious for you to kill this nigga. Come on cuzzo, please put it down." Jahrome' tone is reasonable and matter of fact. Shaka trembles something awful.

Nyeema snaps. Her mouth twitches when she hiss, "You don't tell me shit. Don't tell me what to do."

Jahrome sniffs his lip, pokes his chest out, and raises his nose. Whether or not he is afraid, he won't fold to his fear. What he doesn't realize is that Nyeema ' mind has been overthrown by venomous beings. Their voices howl, whisper, and shrill for her to kill. The more she disobeys their commands the greater the agony she endures. But, slowly she fights against them, weakly. Like a trainee that lifts weights even when their arms are shaking and their muscles are collapsing. She fights back. Slobber streams her bottom lip. She moves like a malfunctioning robot. Seeing this Jahrome decides to take a different approach.

"Drop the Fucking knife Nyeema ." Jahrome' young voice roars over the racy Meek Mill 'Lord Knows'. Though he is fifteen, he has committed himself to be the man of the house in the absence of his daddy.

The knife slips from Nyeema ' hand and she drops right behind it. Her eyes are rolling to the back of her head, her body quakes and jerks from an epileptic spasm. Shaka cries harder.

"Mommy come home, pleasee." He whines.

Jahrome runs to her aide, but he is helpless and confused. "Go get some cold water from the refrigerator and get a clean towel, Shaka." He orders. Shaka flees the room, almost happily dodging Nyeema's quaking body. Jahrome rolls Nyeema on her side, straightens her neck, and lowers the music. Shaka returns with the water and towel.

"Here you go, Jah." He says and bends down at Nyeema ' side. "I'm sorry, Nya." He whispers.

"Shut your ass up, that's what your playful ass get for playing too much. You play too much, now move." Jahrome chides.

Shaka abides, but pouts, "Shut up punk."

Nyeema is spaced out. A powerful unseen force yanks her downward at the speed of two hundred miles per hour minimum she clashes into a zero degree atmosphere. She imagines herself reincarnated as an ice glacier only to be broken as she ascends deeper into a total sea of darkness inside of a floorless ocean. She is so afraid that she may disappear completely that she surrenders to the enraged tidal waves. From vapor she rises onto a plateau in the center of an ancient forest's clearing. Birds chirp and echo eerie cackles. An owl nearly soars through her. As it passes her by she hears its breathing flow and its serene heartbeat. Beginning to believe that she is lost in the maze of a haunted dream, she panics. Searching for a way out she runs down the plateau, but halts by the sight of an Akhal Teke foal whose metallic sheen mesmerizes her. The beautiful foal bows to her with saddened eyes. The foal leans on her. She rubs its cheek and pat its back. A single tear rolls from its right eye. Nyeema relates to the loneliness that becomes a child that has lost her mother. Her mother passed away when Nyeema was only six years old. An unamendable void will forever yearn for that missing piece to her heart. Then, out of thin air, a fully grown Akhal Teke, golden metallic sheen with splashes of black, trots from the opposite end of the forest's clearing. It embraces its young, forehead to forehead. It signals the foal to follow her. The fully grown Akhal Teke heads for the forest, its flowing black and gold mane sways in the wind gracefully. The foal trots behind its mother with the same endurance of speed and grace, just a smaller version. Onward, they disappear and their galloping fades in the distance. The ground is quaking. The solid land fades into charcoal dust. Nyeema is lodged into its whirlwind. She tries to recite her psalms, but her breath is sucked away. The ultralight beams and enhances her vibrational frequency. She is a vessel of light. She is a moving conscience with no need for breath and oxygen. Neon colors igniting into geometrical shapes allure her. She rises up from the den of the ultralight beam' pool of freezing cold water.

Nagaa Ra greets her. "There are worlds they have not told you about. You will soon realize you are not dreaming, then you'll know that you can leave your mind and live ever and ever. Elevate your cells."

Nyeema is spooked. His demeanor is super powerful. His voice of thunder. Two of his long locs hang out of his dazzling hood. A gold bead shines on the right loc. Everything about his appearance is intriguing yet terrifying. He is grandiose in stature.

"Who, who is you? Why do I keep coming here?"

"That's for you to learn. When you're ready the knowledge will come"

"This doesn't make sense. I feel like I'm losing my mind."

"Lose your mind. Lose what has it you must lose."

Nyeema is floored. This unknown creature is speaking to her as if he knows her better than she knows herself. "Who are you?" Nyeema nearly begs.

"I am Nagaa Ra. Brother of the wind. Father of myths."

Nyeema is ready to scream. Nothing is making sense anymore. She had grown comfortable being the outcast. The fine gorgeous girl who boys liked and pretended to not feel her based on fear of being clowned. She's never made friends easily. Her aunty Kem is her closest confidant, and on troubled days she converse with the night sky in hopes that her mother hears her. Now her world is crumbling down. The weed, the voices, merged with the sudden vivid dreamlike experiences. She can't phantom her life tumbling out of control any further. She is naked when she steps out of the pool, and covers herself with blistering speed.

"If only you knew the spiritual meaning of your temple's anatomy. You would have no shame. Garments are merely cosmetic. I am behooved to aware you, earthly one." Nagaa Ra says, a sense of sarcastic irritation strokes his delivery. Nagaa Ra flickers a magical appealing dust onto Nyeema. A red and shimmering-bronze, futuristic, kaftan cloths her. Bewildered and amazed, she touches the fabric and admires its dynamite design.

Nagaa chuckles. "You earthbound creature, you carry your vain conditions wherever you travel." Says Nagaa Ra.

The cadence of his speech reminds her of the actor James Earl Jones but with a thunderous southern drawl. "Your kind tickles me. You cherish everything about your cells. You are so possessive of all that the hands can feel and the eyes can see, but you have no loyalty to your soul and no desire to impress your spirit." Nagaa Ra continues.

Nyeema does not comprehend his meaning. She is far from the shallow materialistic teenager that is common among her peers. Instead of just calling her a human, he calls her an earthbound. His way with words is far too extra. She would be less confused if he communicated to her through simpler terms. Nagaa Ra tells her to grab on to him. She realizes how massive the one room is. It is as wide and grand as the sky. Nagaa Ra soars through the massive space of ultralight with Nyeema holding onto him. He informs her that there is a special welcoming ritual to be held by their nation in her honor. Nyeema heart skips a beat. An intense feeling of anxiety surrounds her. She is frightened. In total panic that she may be trapped on this odd planet forever.

Nagaa Ra speaks in his language of three vowels, *o, u, and e.* A flying saucer soars like a turbocharged boomerang into the lair of beaming light. Like an airplane the saucer appears tiny at a far distance, but is actually grand in size and weight up close. The saucer makes noise that sounds like bad radio feedback, then a door opens on the bottom. Nagaa Ra lifts Nyeema into his arms, his wings flex slightly as he charges into the saucer at an impossible speed. At the speed of light they land on an island with a fruit punch colored ocean. Eighteen creatures resembling the male and female version of Nagaa Ra stand over a blazing stone fire on the silver sand. Large charcoal cones. Nagaa still holds Nyeema in his arms as they exit the saucer and approach the ritualist. Their blue eyes and dark-bluish skin send cutting chills up her spine. Sa Nut is the first to step away from the semi-circle. As much as these creatures look similar there are subtle yet visible distinctions between them. Sa Nut has a nose ring whereas Nagaa Ra doesn't. She purplish locs with several beads. Nagaa has one golden bead on one hanging loc. He is a head taller than she is. Her voice is also thunderous, still somehow feminine.

"We knew if you returned that you were truly our lost starseed, quod mythicon anathema." Sa Nut whispers into Nyeema' ear. "The soul never really leaves its home." Sa Nut says. Nagaa Ra releases Nyeema into Sa Nut' arms. Innately Nyeema rests her head on Sa Nut' bosom as she walks her to the crown of the semi-circle.

"You are not the only lost seed. Your sister borders the portal that leads her home, but she does not have the same courage as you." Sa Nut says. Nyeema's heart slams against her rib cage. She was aware that she was not her father's only child. But the fact that they may be closer than she thinks moves her to a level of overwhelming emotion she has never known. This weird place that welcomes her weird self may bring her closer to her long lost sister. Shaken, she quiets her anxiety by pushing herself to believe they may not mean her blood sister on earth, maybe they mean her sister that is not an actual sister but just another starseed, whatever that means.

A choir of hums rattle the ground beneath the sand. Crows emerge on the shoulders of each female. The males fold into a scorpion sitting position. The humming continues. One of the statuesque females steps out of the circle and offers Nyeema a plate of Black Sapote. Nyeema bites into the ripe fruit and is pleased with its chocolate pudding texture. The fruit has an intoxicating effect. Nyeema feels high. Her body sways and rocks without her doing. Sa Nut Walks empress to the fire. Nyeema resists and screams to be let go. Just as she thinks she is being thrown into the fire she rises like a phoenix levitating above the giant suspicious creatures.

'You are an ocean of emotion. Stop resisting. Relax." Sa Nut tells Nyeema. They are eye to eye. Nagaa Ra begins playing a drum with his hands.

"The urge to know who we are. Overflows you. But the answers are already within you." Nagaa Ra says. "But let us formally introduce us. We are Daemons. Beacons of the world of above moons. Terra Supra Neomenia. Our native tongue is Latin. Our region is on the southern layer. We see that you are not prepared to take place on your square here. But we have great faith that our knowledge and belief of your ability will come into fruition one day soon. In great faith my people ask that you rise up Nyeema. Surge sursus. Rise up." Nagaa Ra proclaims with godlike conviction.

The rest of the Daemons join in, chanting along with Nagaa Ra and Sa Nut. *Surge sursus. Surge sursus. Surge sursus.* The more they chant for Nyeema to rise up, the higher she elevates above them. The horizon changes into a lime and golden color. Nyeema emerges into its abyss.

"Arisen your senses" They speak to her in synchronicity. She wells up with an emotion rising from her core. An emotion that is felt only when she visualizes what could and would be if she was to ever miraculously reunite with her mother. It is a wondrous serene feeling. Then everything explodes. Darkness takes over. She is lost in a world of water. Compelled by an unseen force so powerful and supernaturally fast.

"I could die like this." Nyeema says to herself. Her voice echoes and ripples. She is ready to surrender when her breath becomes light and she feels herself lying on a smooth surface. The sound of waves pushing against the wind astounds her. She inhaled the scent of salted water and raw plants. She opens her eyes and is exposed to a Jurassic park type scenery. She is on dry land but her surroundings are mostly grandiose trees and boundless water.

"Let's play a game." The voice of an unknown female being rattled through the light breeze like nature's own surround sound. Nyeema's state of calmness subsides. She is alert and ready to take flight. Slowly she looks from left to right as she lays in the sand. Then a massive figure soars down and swoops Nyeema into her bosom. Nyeema freezes in terror. There is no sense in putting up a fight. Her opponent is a giant. Nyeema does not measure up to a fraction of the humongous woman's palm. The woman stretches as long as the sea. Her aura is cool and enchanting.

"My name Yemaya, what's your name?" She asks Nyeema in a lighthearted manner.

Nyeema gives a trembling response. "Ny-ny-eema."

"Ooh that's almost like my name. We are twins, aren't we?"

Nyeema is quiet. The whole situation is creeping her out. Silence is the only way she could appear to be calm.

"I'm sorry, Nyeema. I know you must be very afraid. I'm so huge. I'm made up of nature's most powerful elements. Air and water. Everyone needs me but no one ever plays with me. I get so bored sometimes."

"Where are you taking me?"

"Oh, sorry. You don't wanna play with me?"

"I wanna go home."

"Hmph, fine. I don't need you. I don't need anybody. Everyone needs me, but nobody loves me. Nobody ever wants to play with me."

Nyeema is terrified and annoyed at the sametime. Yemaya is so childish and needy, she thinks.

"Well then bye." Yemaya says, then throws Nyeema so hard that she is thrusted into the abyss of the sea. Nyeema prepares for the rapture, but is met with the sweet bliss of serenity. She stops resisting and swims effortlessly through the boundless sea.

"Nyeema, the great one." A cute feminine voice resounds easily throughout the sea. A beautiful girl around the same age as Nyeema levitates hundreds of yards away, but Nyeema sees her clearly from where she hovers.

"How do you know my name?" Nyeema asks.

"Everyone knows your name, you're a myth to many but your name is spoken throughout every corner of the omniverse."

"In what way? Why?"

"You possess powers and gifts you refuse to embrace. You are a goddess Nyeema. You are a ruler of many, but you play small and stifle your abilities."

"I must watch too much fucking Anime because this can't be life."

The girl laughed heartily. "It is beyond life. It is beyond you or me." The girl zoomed at the speed of life and was face to face with Nyeema in a matter of seconds. She continued, " I will anchor you, but the power is in your hands."

"What are you talking about?"

"I'll show you." The girl said, then hugged Nyeema close. They vanished from the ocean and ended up in a beautiful castlesque home. The home was full of flowers, plants, herbs, stones, crystals, gems, and other essentials that promoted healing and high vibrations. The girl led Nyeema up the spiraling stairs. The girl stopped at a door and knocked. A woman with skin as black as coal and locs that hung to the floor opened the door.

She smiled revealing a mouth filled with gold teeth. "Finally. I thought you'd take another eternity."Nyeema and the girl towered over the woman, but she was not one to intimidate.

"Everything's ready." The woman said. She gestured for Nyeema and the girl to sit around a potion pot. The woman and the girl took turns drinking the potion from a serving spoon. Nyeema was cautious, but the fact that they drank from the same pot which they offered her was quite calming. She drank the potion and was surprised at its sweet goodness.

The woman smiled and clapped her hands. "You are the perfect one, Nyeema."

Nyeema was underwhelmed. She wanted to go home. She missed her family. She was tired of those trippy outer body experiences. Whoever those odd creatures thought she was made her uncomfortable. She didn't feel powerful. She knew she was unique, but everybody was if they would just admit it and be themselves. That didn't make her a goddess-like being, it made her an individual. "What if I'm not who you think I am? What if you have the wrong girl?"

"If you were the wrong girl you'd be dead by now. That potion is to poison all imposters, but it was nothing but a fruity nectar to you."

"Okay what does it mean? What now? I just wanna go home. I wanna wake up from all of this."

"Then surrender, embrace the wonders of the omniverse. Once you unbound your mind, your true power will be unleashed."

"How do I do that?"

"Stop asking how and go within. The keys are within you."

"You have to quiet your mind. Relinquish all doubts. Breathe. Be light as a feather."

Nyeema followed the girl's instructions and took slow deep breaths. Her breaths flowed effortlessly. Waves of peace and serenity vibrated through her until she evaporated from the woman and the girl's presence. She emerged upon a cliff where she faced the backs of two feminine creatures with massive angelic wings. Their garments were white as snow. Each of their hair was cornrowed into the one long plait that flowed between the breasts of their wings. Nyeema realized that she was no longer in the flesh. She was free from the shell of her body. Yet she still beheld her senses. She was no longer in human form, but they still saw her. It was her mother and grandmother. They said nothing, but together they handed Nyeema a round gold plated box. Nyeema's spirit bowed and a gate opened within the sky. Her mother and grandmother flew away. The gates closed and vanished into the sky. Nyeema opened the box and the entire atmosphere became a blinding fierce light.

***

Kemet prayed with all her might as she sat next to Nyeema's hospital bed. Nyeema opened her eyes at the voice of her weary aunt: "God I shall not fear, for I know you are with me. I give you my trust. I put my faith in you. Whatever is afflicting my niece dear God I pray that you destroy it and renew this child's life…" It had been seven days. Nyeema was hooked up to tubes and I.v's.

"Auntie." Nyeema said drowsily.

"Nyeema, niece. Baby I thought I lost you." Kemet sobbed as she hugged Nyeema. "God is so good." She cried. Nyeema felt relieved, she hugged her auntie tight and sighed gratefully.

The doctors ran several tests on Nyeema before she was discharged. As soon as Nyeema and Kemet entered the house they were met with loud music and Jahrome and Shaka playing the playstation 4 in the living room.

"Nyeema, what up cuz?!" Shaka screamed and ran to hug her happily. Jahrome joined them.

"Dang cuz, you had us scared. Don't ever do that again." Jahrome said.

Later that night they sat around, ate ribs and watched Bad Boys For Life. They were just happy to be reunited. They were unaware that Nyeema possessed powers to read their minds, to heal, and bring someone back to life from a simple touch. They were unaware of her new purpose on earth, but she vowed to never scare them again. She was in control of this go around.

Made in the USA
Columbia, SC
21 February 2021